Heart
My Suitcase

Deepti Singh Gupta did her graduation and post-graduation from Hindu College, Delhi University, and has a doctorate in botany. She gave up a career in academia to pursue her two main passions—writing and travel. She set up a travel blog in 2013 and now is an avid blogger *@GlobalPitara*.

Her columns and photographs have been featured in magazines and websites such as *Lonely Planet* and *National Geographic*. She has also exhibited her travel photographs at prestigious art galleries. She lives in Faridabad, with her son Kushagra and her lawyer husband Jeetender.

This is her debut novel.

My Suitcase Heart

DEEPTI SINGH GUPTA

RUPA

Published by
Rupa Publications India Pvt. Ltd 2021
7/16, Ansari Road, Daryaganj
New Delhi 110002

Sales Centres:
Allahabad Bengaluru Chennai
Hyderabad Jaipur Kathmandu
Kolkata Mumbai

Copyright © Deepti Singh Gupta 2021

This is a work of fiction. Names, characters, places and incidents are either the product of the author's imagination or are used fictitiously and any resemblance to any actual person, living or dead,
events or locales is entirely coincidental.

All rights reserved.
No part of this publication may be reproduced, transmitted, or stored in a retrieval system, in any form or by any means, electronic, mechanical, photocopying, recording or otherwise, without the prior permission of the publisher.

ISBN: 978-93-91256-04-3

First impression 2021

10 9 8 7 6 5 4 3 2 1

The moral right of the author has been asserted.

Printed at Thomson Press India Ltd., Faridabad

This book is sold subject to the condition that it shall not, by way of trade or otherwise, be lent, resold, hired out, or otherwise circulated, without the publisher's prior consent, in any form of binding or cover other than that in which it is published.

For my twinkling star—Badi Mummy

Thank you
For the goodbye note that was never sent
The wet towel, again, on the floor …
That suitcase full of memories,
Aside, in the corner
Waiting to explode—yet shy
Like an unsure bride standing at the altar …
Thank you for no locks in there
I pick up the frayed yellow diary
Holding on to a hope so huge
I pluck out that rose; our rose
The petals have withered away, only stains remain
Like eraser marks on inked sheets …
That thorn still remembers to prick
Thank you for the thorn, my love
For, now I know, my heart still bleeds!

Prologue

They had been sailing for six days when they heard the rumours. Something unsettling about a new sort of virus that had taken the world by storm, a pandemic in the making, a threat to lives across the globe. By the time the evening rolled in, their worst fears were confirmed.

The flu-like virus had spread, much like wildfire, and the infection was highly contagious with the mortality rate soaring. While they were still trying to make sense of this revelation and the threat it posed, the passengers were asked to stay inside their cabins till further notice. Chaos and panic ensued.

Venice in Italy was to be where they set port and embarked, but as the news had it, it was now a hotbed of this contagious new disease called coronavirus—Covid-19. All the cruise passengers were suspected carriers of the infection, which apparently took anywhere between seven and fourteen days to show any symptoms. The PA system on the ship was working overtime even as they tried to get a grip on the whole situation and process what lay ahead of them. Left with no option but to follow the myriad instructions, the group retired for the day, though it was Ahana and Aadi's balcony suite that they all scrambled in. Zorawar and Mayank had enough sense to grab some munchies and beers to keep spirits high. They sat there, the gang, huddled in a room like old times, only the atmosphere of the room was thick with tension and anxiety unlike earlier. The pack never failed to attract trouble, this brigade of school friends, notorious for snafus and misadventures, but this time the reunion seemed to be star-crossed from the word go.

The following days were hazy, like a nightmare; all cruisers still at sea were forcibly confined to their respective cabins. Their activities were restricted, the common areas remained closed; they were just a bunch of prisoners at sea, quarantined as suspect carriers of an incurable, fatal disease. The servers and the crew, meanwhile, diligently carried on with their duties, providing them with basic amenities which, however, were fast depleting in stock. Ostensibly, the scheduled itinerary had been abandoned since none of the listed ports allowed the ship to dock. They were stranded on the high seas with nothing to do but wait endlessly. As time passed, the rooms were not being cleaned, toiletries not being replenished, food supply to the rooms was sporadic; the holiday had turned into a living hell, they were like on a floating concentration camp. Mahi did not want to encourage Ahana's theory of the group being jinxed but she was herself beginning to wonder.

Prologue

They constantly touched base with each other through it all. Drifty, the on-board communication app that Samar had developed for the cruise liner kept them tethered.

'Thank God for it,' Mahi said, mouthing a silent prayer. 'Samar' … with so many years between them, a chasm beyond countries and decades splitting them apart, her heart still picked a beat on his mention. She could do anything to rewrite her history, her story with him, of what could have been.

With endless hours to while away and nothing much to do, Mahi's thoughts meandered to the time gone by. She had always been an overthinker, she was a Virgo but with all traits of a Gemini, she could be two people in two different places and do justice to both. She had dreams and stories, a trunk full of memories and a suitcase full of hope. She lived in two worlds, in yesterday even as she spread her wings to the new tomorrow, a time traveller of sorts… And now somehow she had managed to reach the 1990s, of India, of home.

The Invite

2019

The phone beeps. Mayank peeps through half-open eyes, a long poem by Ahana.

> 'Remember?
> When You and I were little kids,
> When realities hadn't dawned upon us,
> Responsibilities we didn't know.
> We wandered aimlessly, surveying the new building around the corner
> Or making friends with a stray dog.
> Remember?
> The toffees we shared and the ones we didn't,
> The games we played and the ones we didn't.
> Things changed.
> Times changed.
> We grew up and so did our distances.

The footprints we had left on the rain-soaked mud faded away,
And, so did our togetherness.
Today we stand apart,
A wide chasm staring at us,
We are like banks of a river,
Originating together and parted Forever…
Remember Me??'

He tosses to the other side and pulls the blanket up his head, irritated by the influx of messages on this new chat group that Ahana had sprung up with. The barrage of messages forces him to take another look.

A plan is being made, some reunion of sorts. Mayank isn't interested; he doesn't have the time or the inclination. There was a time when he couldn't do without meeting these people even for a single day, sharing pizza and Campa Colas at Delish Delights after their tuitions. They were once his people, his friends, his hangout buddies, his lifelines. But that had changed many moons ago. His tethers had gradually weakened and had all gotten lost in the intricate mesh that time had woven around him.

Poorvi snuggled closer to him.

'Who are you chatting with at this hour?' she quizzed sleepily. Mayank quietly handed over the phone for her to read the chat. She plumped up her pillow to adjust her head and put her glasses on.

The Invite

'Why have I not been added to this group yet?' she cribbed characteristically. Mayank shrugged, he cared two hoots.

'We should go,' she added, seeming excited to Mayank.

Ahana and Aadi were celebrating their tenth anniversary. They had booked suites in a cruise across the Mediterranean and were begging (even emotionally blackmailing) them all to join. Ahana had always been overindulgent, even preposterous, but she still was the fulcrum to their group, the binding force that kept them looping together.

Mayank wasn't interested though, he had more important things to do in life, his merchant banking job didn't leave him with much time and he was glad for that.

'We are going, it will do us both good. And we haven't met any of them for ages, wonder how they are doing.' Poorvi had made the decision almost unilaterally, but then it was always like this or else a fight ensued. Mayank did not have the energy to fight.

'What about your pledge to take flights only when absolutely necessary', he tried to reason.

'This is important, meeting old friends, reliving those moments, being young again.' Poorvi was flushing with excitement. Mayank didn't want to relive anything, he didn't want to meet old friends, he didn't want any of this … but he did not want another argument to boil up. He yielded easily and surrendered as usual.

Mahi kept a tight schedule and was returning from an assignment in Bruges, now heading towards Colmar in

France after a short hop in Zurich and thereafter, Montreux. Bruges the chocolate box town of Belgium. 'What a beautiful, quaint, charming city with cobblestone streets, canals, cute little souvenir shops, chic restaurants and teeming tourists,' she mused as images of Bruges played in her mind like a montage. She had found the town very walkable and yet the horse-carriage ride around the fairy-tale town was something she could not miss for the world along with the amazing hot chocolate and waffles that it was so famous for. She had found a story for her next article, apparently, the famous Madonna and Child, carved in Italy, was bought by a Bruges merchant, Alexander Mouscron, and donated in 1514 to the Church of Our Lady in Bruges. It is the only sculpture by Michelangelo that left Italy during his lifetime. The sculpture was stolen in 1794 and later returned only to disappear a second time during the Nazi regime.

Mahi lingered a little as the light changed, she had come a long way from the bucolic vistas of the enchanting Lake Geneva ensconced by the terraced vineyards of Lausanne; her mind was now wandering off, beyond the uninspiring views of the A9 Toll Road to the lanes bursting with a riot of fiery red gulmohars back in India. The wanderlust for all things novel, the aim to ditch the cookie-cutter holiday and explore uncharted territories, was why she was heading towards the Alsace Wine Route in France famous for its lush vineyards, formidable castles and colourful half-timbered houses, besides, obviously, the French wine. She had during one of her travel research expeditions discovered this quaint town called Colmar which had a rivulet running down in the middle of the old town and bordered with colourful Tudor style gingerbread houses and boutiques. The bustling centre looked like a scene straight out of Venice, thus and therefore, the town was also known as Petite Venezia aka Little Venice. Colmar was the central hub from where the romantic wine route, covering some of the most beautiful villages of Europe in the Alsace region of France, could be covered. The familiar feeling of excitement to see and discover a new foreign town was building up inside her as she drew closer. She pressed onwards to Colmar diligently following signs for Mulhouse/France/Flughafen. Though the snow was confined to the shoulders of the highway, an hour's drive from Montreux to Colmar was taking forever because of road closure on A35 near Basel. Mahi was not complaining, she needed to collect her thoughts before she reached anywhere. Her heart was in a flutter since Ahana's message showed up on her phone.

Samar had initially resisted his sister Ahana's plan for a reunion on her tenth wedding anniversary. He was well aware of his sibling's scheming and was a little wary of her sudden enthusiasm and zeal, but finally, he caved in. He did need some time away, and it would do Kian a great deal of good to bond with his family.

Kian was too young to fathom loss, but he did miss his mom. 'Ahana's proximity might fill that void, even if it was only for a few days,' Samar pondered. Besides, he could work out a good deal with the cruise liner since he had recently developed an app for them. His app, Drifty, was a novel idea and it facilitated on-board communication between passengers without any data charges; calls, as well as chats through the mobiles, were possible via the app and apparently, the shipping company was quite happy with the results.

Meanwhile, a new unknown number had been added to the chat group Ahana had created ... Ishiqa was back in the fold.

Part 1
THE CLIQUE

Mahi & Samar

High School
Winter
Mid-1990s

They were the star couple at their school. He fitted the TDH parameters (tall, dark and handsome for the uninitiated) like a dream and she, well, she was the dream. 'Your deep green eyes and thick brown mane are enough to capture and captivate an entire regiment—and these are just gullible schoolboys,' Ahana often joked.

A million hearts broke when she first started dating Samar. Some remained hopeful, for Mahi never stuck around a boy for too long. 'This mushy-mushy romance smothers me,' she had confided to Ahana once. 'Pesky', was the term she often used for all the boys she had dumped, and that it was an art she thought she had mastered—until Samar.

Samar, meanwhile, was smart enough to take 'insider tips' from Ahana, his little twin sister (seniority counts, even if it is only marked by a couple of minutes). What were a few chocolates and some gruelling homework, when in lieu he was getting to know Mahi up close. He had always been besotted with her, but had hidden it too well. He was way out of her league.

For Mahi, he was just one among the gang, a clique that everyone else in the school envied, a group that was as notorious among peers for mischief as it was popular amongst the teachers. Mahi saw nothing more than a friend in Samar, or so he thought as she laughed at his acts: spoofs he made on the life sketches of great men, or when he pulled an act on yet another unsuspecting teacher. Soon they were sharing jokes and gossip, and now, sometimes lunch too. He would do her maths homework and show her how to use the computers (yes, computer were the new thing then, requiring special rooms, bare feet entry and fixed slots). She would tear up his graphs and use them for her own home-work while he would be punished for his incomplete work. She would hide his notebooks, and they would be ordered to stand outside the classroom together (if only the teacher knew that it wasn't a punishment but a reward). She would now share Hershey's kisses with him and insist that he read a Mills & Boon she had enjoyed (Mills & Boon for god's sake, which boy in his right mind would read that?) and he still thought—'if only'.

Theirs wasn't the love-at-first-sight kind of romance; no thunderstorms struck when they met, but it was love—a love that grows organically. A hesitant drizzle, which slowly develops into a steady shower.

The hints started becoming more explicit and soon, he realized that the 'if only' was 'very possible'. It was slow, but he won her over. Not with flowers and chocolates, but with humour and wit. He was okay with slow.

Sweaty palms soon walked hand in hand past wild fields and flaming trees.

Two teenagers, hearts racing, passions soaring ... it happened. It had to happen; they were meant to be. He remembered it like yesterday. They kissed while the birds chirped, while the clouds meandered to the other end, while the sun bid farewell to the rosy sky. They kissed while the world went by. The beating of their hearts like music made in heaven.

Ishiqa, Poorvi & Mayank

High School
Mid-1990s

'Ma'am, may I come in?' Ishiqa or Ish (as she was nicknamed) extended her arm to seek permission. It was her first day at the new school. Her dad had been transferred yet again and they, had to move base in the middle of the semester.

The class was suddenly unusually quiet; the girls were busy sizing her up and the boys, well, the boys were busy sizing her up.

Grewal Ma'am welcomed the new student and introduced her to the class. She pointed to the empty seat beside Mayank. Poorvi hadn't come to school that day, and thus, Ish occupied Poorvi's coveted front row seat, by fluke.

Aadi pinched Mayank from under the bench. 'You lucky @#@##,' he mouthed the words. Mayank grinned from ear to ear. His skin tingled as Ish's hand accidentally touched his while reaching for the stylo. Mayank sent a silent 'thank you'

Ishiqa, Poorvi & Mayank

in his head to Poorvi for being sick and away.

Ishiqa was pretty with her dark hair and her doe-shaped eyes; a shining example of classic timeless beauty. Her smile reached her eyes and obviously, Mayank, like many other naive teenage hearts, fell for it instantly. Maybe, she didn't completely realize the effect she had on boys.

The classroom suddenly felt charged. The boys were at their best behaviour the entire day and the girls, sensing some tough competition, were trying hard to be extraordinarily affable. Ish made several friends that day and it was a shame when the final bell rang and everybody had to bid each other goodbye.

Mayank could not stop thinking about her all day. School had suddenly become the most important part of his day and his life. He was dying to tell Poorvi all about it, but that would have to wait until Poorvi awoke from her slumber. Her grandmother was not in any mood to disturb her darling angel who had slept after such difficulty, all thanks to a bad throat and a runny nose. Mayank was not listening to the details Poorvi so zealously gave him when he called to check on her.

He spent hours watching the sunlight dance across the faded wooden shutters in his room. For the first time, he noticed how the stars slowly gathered to embellish the sky; the chitter-chatter of birds returning to their nests after dark was music to him that day. His heart was somewhere in the land of cascading waterfalls and melting glaciers.

He was doped on love.

'Cool your jets, will you,' Mayank admonished his restless self. He scrubbed himself excessively in the shower the next morning and jangled his head twice on the tap while picking up the rogue soap bar. But he was undeterred. 'No milk today, mom,' he shouted as he pedalled out on his bicycle.

The air was crisp and the wildflowers were bobbing their heads in unison as he accelerated towards the school.

Poorvi was already there when he entered the class. And, she was throwing an unprecedented fit.

Her backpack had been ceremoniously dumped on the ground, her hands were in the air. She was churning out swear words by the dozen. Ish sat there, frozen. She was not a timid girl but the barrage of insults that came hurtling towards her was something she was unfamiliar with.

Mayank moved swiftly, coming between his two girls. 'Hey, Poorvi, how are you feeling today? the extra zing in his voice didn't go unnoticed, but the sugarcoating had no effect. Poorvi was in no mood to relent. 'No one,' a voice screamed in her head, none had the audacity to replace her. "This new girl—whatever her name was, Ishiqa, huh, or whatever—how dare she take my seat, my place, beside Mayank?"

'Just get up, right this second,' she yelled. Ish seemed intimidated, a little flustered, yet unobliging. Mayank took Poorvi's hand and gave it a tight squeeze. 'Poorvi, Poorv, c'mon. She didn't choose to sit here. Ma'am wanted her to sit in the front to ensure that she makes up for lost time and can

Ishiqa, Poorvi & Mayank

understand better. Don't be so hard on her. She will switch places once she gets into the groove, I promise,' Mayank said beseechingly, almost begging on Ish's behalf.

Poorvi could see it in his eyes. Mayank was sold. One day, she skipped school for one single day and Mayank was gone, gone from being hers to being someone she didn't recognize any more.

But she would not give him away with such ease. She would fight. Ish might have taken her bench, but she would not take away what was hers. Mayank was hers. Mayank was for Poorvi, and Poorvi could kill to prove that.

'Peace?' Mayank grinned sheepishly.

Poorvi managed to feign a smile.

Reluctantly, she walked to the back of the classroom, Mayank gleefully carrying her bag to her new seat. 'See you at lunch,' he almost tripped while rushing back to Ish. Back at his new favourite bench, he sat down, stole a glance at Poorvi to double check if she was looking; satisfied, he held Ish's hand gently and winked. 'All is good,' he conveyed. She understood and her face relaxed into a tiny smile; his heart exploded into a million pieces. 'That smile can actually make mountains move,' he mused. Meanwhile, Poorvi sat there glum, thinking of the million ways in which she could smash Ish's pretty little face.

Ish joined their group during lunch, almost everybody there had already asked her to join them. Poorvi was fuming, but she knew better than to exhibit her animosity any further.

Manali

High School
Mid-1990s

Mahi could not contain her excitement. They were vacationing in Manali, the Queen of Hills. All her friends were going; Samar would be there too.

The girls could not stop talking about the dresses they were going to bring along. Her hats and shoes were taking up too much space, but she didn't want to leave any behind. She loved accessorizing, and this was her chance to flaunt her style! Seven whole days of respite from her drab school uniform—the shirt tucked in, the skirt sweeping the floor and the mousy buckled shoes.

The boys, well, they were excited too, but they had other things in mind.

Mahi's father kept issuing instructions throughout their drive to school, but was she even listening? 'Call every day. Stay with the group. Don't wander off. Wear sensible shoes while

Manali

hiking, and please, stay away from treacherous cliffs. Have you kept all your medicines? And don't eat roadside food.' It was like a manual. Mahi just kept nodding absentmindedly.

The size of her suitcase did lift some initial eyebrows, but soon, Ish's and Ahana's skybags diverted attention from her relatively smaller baggage. They would need personal coolies for all the stuff they seemed to be carrying. The boys, meanwhile, gladly came to assist and soon they were settled in the Volvo bus, adjusted into temporary seating arrangements for the benefit of the parents' peace of mind. The atmosphere was eclectic; packs of chips soon began to circulate, antakshari rounds (cliché, but a staple for every group journey) had already started, jokes were being cracked.

After an hour or more of cacophony and chaos—luggage shuffling and seat swapping—they settled into a calm bonhomie as the bus manoeuvred through the traffic of city after city. They had to make a lot of pit stops—one or the other students suddenly and urgently had to pee and a couple of them were dealing with strong bouts of motion sickness. It was a long way to Manali, they realized.

Samar was now sitting next to Mahi. 'What are you listening to?' he asked. Mahi handed the Walkman over. 'Fast Car' by Tracy Chapman was playing.

'Isn't it ... like ... old?' His tone verged on mocking.

'Shh, just listen,' Mahi mouthed softly. The song no longer sounded old, it felt now ... them.

They travelled through the night, and they finally checked

into the hotel past dinner the next day, completely exhausted. Four students each in a room was the arrangement. They had a hard time convincing Mr Singh, their teacher-in-charge, that the five girls wanted to be in the same room. Exasperated and tired, Mr Singh finally caved in. Mahi, Ahana, Poorvi, Ishiqa and Hiya were together. Fitting in was difficult, especially since half the space was taken by their superfluous luggage. The four of them cramped together on the bed while Hiya volunteered to take the mattress on the floor (the extra bed could not be accommodated for obvious reasons). Sleep eluded them. Was it exertion or the excitement of this trip? No one could tell. They could hear the muffled conversations of the boys next door; Mahi strained to hear if she could recognize the voices in the adjacent room; she hoped it was Samar and the rest, but it was a long shot.

Morning was chaotic. Getting ready in the tiny bathroom, each waiting for a turn, was no easy task, and finding stuff in the busy room was harder still. Ish was in a glum mood, dissatisfied with her winged eyeliner. Ahana was focused on ironing her dress and Poorvi was taking forever in the shower. Hiya was the only one who looked calm, bathed and ready, unsuccessfully trying to tidy the mess the room was in.

The glances they got from the boys while descending the stairs made up for all the hard work they had put in; some of the other girls looked unhappy though, and that made the four feel even better. The view outside was breathtaking; the hotel was set in a picture-postcard location—a stream gurgling in

Manali

its backyard, tree boughs drooping with the weight of ripe-red apples, dazzling mountains beckoning them to venture out. The tranquillity was only broken by the chirping of birds and buzzing of pesky insects flitting around from flower to flower.

The setting was absolutely hypnotic. Mahi fell in love. This was her first tryst with wanderlust, and she was smitten. Years later, in another decade, Mahi would slowly graduate from being a tourist, trying to pin all the must-visit places across the globe on her wall, far removed from being the timorous traveller, teetering after city guidebooks and GPS commands, from completely ignoring the smorgasbord of cultures, of romance, of epicurean delight and street-food staples that a place, any place has to offer, to becoming a traveller who gets truly lost in the mishmash of the kitsch and the aesthetic, a lover of the footnotes and footpaths—unravelling, discovering, unearthing real treasures, savouring moments, tasting travel, living the journey and making stories. Mahi would carry her suitcase around the world in search of places, of people, of home, of belonging, and with it all will travel her heart.

But that is a story for another time.

The breakfast spread at the hotel was lavish: Spanish omelette, toast with butter and jam, aloo paratha, tea and juice. The din of excited jibber-jabber made it all look even more promising. They were going rafting that day! Fear, excitement and the adrenaline rush was so tangible that Mahi could feel blood pumping through her ears. 'I could get addicted to this feeling,' she thought.

Rain pattered down throughout the short drive to the rafting site, the silver clouds seemed to have swilled more liquor than they could contain, and their path snaked through kaleidoscopic vistas of lush mountains. And then, they came across this breathtaking white waterfall, cascading down the glistening rocks, then came yet another bigger shower, catapulting down like white foam on molten copper and thereafter ... and thereafter, the count did not stop.

They all looked the same now with their lifejackets and helmets on, as they clumsily climbed atop the kayaking raft. Being on the same boat with Samar was comforting, but why did the blood rush twice as fast to her head?

'A rapid is coming, everybody duck,' shouted the guide.

He even had a name for this rapid. Curiously, all the rapids along their way had been christened. They viewed the enormous white wall approaching them, just moments before it thrashed against their boat and they were all sucked in by the gargantuan wave—the raft hurled in all directions. The only thing that kept them glued to the kayak were the ropes on the side to which they held on to for dear life; thank god they had heard the instructions carefully.

The raft journey continued for three whole hours, starting with a Class 3 Rapid, navigating through a Class 2 and finally, the big, Class 1. The river looked beautiful on the course: dazzling, the smooth rocks below clearly visible. Mahi finally noticed it once their tryst with the raging waves ended. Her muscles ached as she frantically paddled the raft in sync with

Manali

the others. She didn't understand how it helped when the waves surged in the way they did. She and Hiya stayed aboard while most others jumped off the raft in search of calmer waters. It was a dip too many, no thanks!

The girls gave a pass to the Rappelling Adventure too; the heat was overbearing as the sun blazed, seemingly too close for comfort. They were ravenous but they had to wait for the boys for their lunch back at the hotel. Rafting had been a thrilling experience, but it was also draining. All this waiting was making them grumpy. Ish almost threw a fit, a flabbergasted Mayank became the unsuspecting target of her outburst when the boys finally trooped back to the bus. But nobody could remain sullen for too long; they all knew that this was precious time: away from home, from school, from scrutiny, with friends, and for some, with sweethearts …

Lunch made things better. Conversation flew over spoonsful of Pahadi chicken, curried beans and roasted cumin baby potatoes. They did fight over bottles of Campa Cola; though supplies were meagre as these beverages were not on the menu and had to be bought with whatever pocket allowance one had. Poorvi was generous in her spending and so they had nothing to worry about per se.

But going back to the room for an afternoon siesta was a mistake. They slept through the evening. Exhaustion finally got the better of them. And so, dinner turned out to be a muted affair—half the troupe didn't turn up, too tired to make the effort. The supervisor too announced his inability to join them for the trip to Rohtang Pass scheduled for the next morning. The other, much junior, teacher would be accompanying (read: chaperoning), they were told. Since the day was to start at five in the morning, the group called it an early night. The pack of cards and the Monopoly board lay untouched in the boys' room ... so much for the plans ...

In the morning they were smothered—from head to toe—in winterwear of all kinds and colours. Mahi wore an electric blue jumpsuit, while Ahana was in a powder pink overcoat. Poorvi was flaunting a down feather jacket her father had couriered from overseas. Ish decided against wearing pink when she saw Ahana, and was now donning a canary yellow topcoat over a cream pullover. Hiya, as usual, was dressed in muted colours but she too seemed ready to brave the chill with a cap and muffler in place. They were going to Rohtang today, which, for most of them, was to be their first rendezvous with snow.

'Ahana, have you brought an extra pair of flat boots? I seem to have only heels on me,' Poorvi called as she frantically searched through her luggage. They all suspected that Poorvi wouldn't have cared to bring any practical shoes with her. Even while rafting, she had to go barefoot for fear of soiling her suede runners.

'Nope,' Ahana replied tartly. She was in no mood to indulge Poorvi—not that she could be of any help—but she certainly wanted to wash her hands off Poorvi's wardrobe woes.

After a good half an hour of—fixing hair, adjusting caps,

putting on lip gloss and mascara—they were finally ready to board the bus. Breakfast was scheduled at the destination itself. Apparently, a full stomach could not survive the treacherous curves en route. The bus ride was traumatic, the terrain perilous with its narrow rutted roads, overlooking steep cliffs while white mist ensnared the crown of the mountains beyond, and the circuitous hairpin loops made their head spin. The entire bus was busy, either praying or throwing up. Mahi too felt squeamish, but she was doing a good job of holding it all together. Hiya was the one getting paler with each passing moment. Mahi nudged Ish, sitting in the aisle seat and closer to Hiya.

'She doesn't look too good,' Mahi whispered.

'Who does?' Ish gesticulated around her, even as the bus bumped forward. 'Hiya? Is all good?' Ish squeezed Hiya's hand.

'I can't breathe,' Hiya gasped.

Ish was worried now and tried to rub Hiya's back fervently.

'Do you have these attacks often ... or is this the first time that you are feeling breathless?' Ish asked in vain, watching as Hiya was evidently struggling for oxygen.

Hiya felt like she was breathing through a squished straw. 'Do you have an inhaler on you?' she wheezed.

Ish and Mahi were in panic mode now. Mahi thought it sensible to approach the teacher accompanying them. They didn't know Ms Dhar too well. She was a junior section teacher but she had seemed friendly and amicable. Not that it mattered in such a grave situation.

My Suitcase Heart

'Ma'am! Ma'am, my friend is apparently having an asthma attack!' Mahi pleaded for her to take over and handle the situation. The teacher seemed as clueless as they had been. She asked the students (some of whom had now gathered to investigate the cause of the commotion) not to crowd around Hiya. She then asked the driver to turn the bus and head to the hotel. The driver, however, explained that it was almost impossible for the bus to take a U-turn here, and that it was better that they reach Rohtang—it was now just a kilometre away. They could then decide.

Meanwhile, Mayank had discovered and borrowed an inhaler, the fellow proprietary student had been reluctant to lend it initially (hygiene issues, you see) but seeing the precariousness of the situation, he caved.

The puff of asthalin was elixir for Hiya, but she still could not breathe freely. The tightness in her chest was excruciating.

They had reached Rohtang. The snow capped peaks were like the tips of harpoons while the milky white clouds mirrored the scattered powdery snow. Sinister freezing winds slapped hard against their bodies as the bus doors opened. It was biting cold and the growling, numbing wind was making things worse. The class made their way towards the snow-festooned hills; meanwhile, Hiya's condition was deteriorating, her breathing jerky, her head dizzy.

Ms Dhar was hoarse shouting at those who had gone ahead of the herd. She had to make a call. Fast. They needed to go back, but a pilot group was already racing to the top.

Manali

The kids seemed unwilling to call off their experience just because one girl was sick. Someone suggested that a few willing students accompany Hiya back; the teacher needed to be with the other students in such a risky landscape. Samar and Aadi volunteered. But some of the girls needed to go with Hiya too, and so, finally, it was Samar, Aadi, Mahi and Ahana who were deputed to escort Hiya back to the hotel.

Obviously, they had to take a local bus. 'I have heard that a drink warms the body. If we can grab something, it might help Hiya until we reach the city,' Aadi suggested. They managed to find a bottle of a local beer from a vendor next to the bus stop (Beer! Yes, only if they had known better). Hiya started to turn blue after two reluctant sips of the awful brew, her limbs numb and her eyelids drooping. Thankfully, the local passengers in the bus were more worldly-wise. One of them snatched the bottle from Ahana's hands, all the while crucifying her with scathing looks. They were asked to throw all their warm jackets over Hiya and rub her hands and feet. Hiya lay on the floor of the bus, disoriented, fighting sleep that threatened to take over. Mahi was constantly calling her name, slapping her hard so she would stay awake. When they realized that they might have made matters worse they were afraid and it was frightening to think of the consequences. The bus was slow and the tumultuous, bumpy journey was a nightmare none of them ever wanted to relive.

Aadi and Samar lifted Hiya up with some help from the

bus conductor and plonked her on the rickshaw. The hospital was just across the road. Mahi made a quick call to the hotel to inform Mr Singh, their teacher-in-charge. Mr Singh was apparently cooped up in his room. He took forever to receive the call at the reception. Once apprised, he expounded on the dos and don'ts and assured them that he would be joining them shortly.

Hiya was administered as many as four injections in the emergency room. Samar filled in the forms while waiting for Mr Singh to take charge. The girls stayed in the room with Hiya once her condition stabilized. The boys returned to the hotel to catch some sleep. Two hours later, Hiya was discharged and they all came back—drained. Mr Singh had excused himself once the situation seemed to be under control.

They were all exhausted beyond words but sleep eluded them. Hiya though, was blissfully slumbering, her face pale but calm. The four of them just sat there, watching her, replaying the horrors of the day and thanking the heavens for miraculously bringing them out of the dark pit they had been thrown into. They were angry too, irked by their selfish mates who chose tobogganing down the snowy slopes over the life of a fellow friend. But then, they were just kids. How else would you excuse handing over a beer for hypoxia? All five of them, unbeknownst to each other, were now bound together by this moment—the shared knowledge of the time they had lived through, the moments filled with shock, pain,

Manali

fear and finally, relief. They were now friends forever.

The rest of the party came back in time for dinner, all of them gushing with excitement, each with a story to tell. But the four were not interested, they had grown up beyond their years in the last few hours, it seemed. Mr Singh didn't hide his displeasure at Ms Dhar's decision to not bring back the entire group as soon as the first signs of trouble had started to show. Ms Dhar would be in deep trouble once they were back at school, Mahi could clearly tell.

It was a new day. The next morning, Ish and Mayank opted to stay back at the hotel with Hiya while the others geared up for a hiking trip, plus a tour of the local Tibetan market (Mahi still has that green and gold, glass bead necklace Samar bought for her from there). The short trek to the hilltop temple was an absolute treat. They plucked juicy apples from the trees, chased butterflies and danced beneath the sundry cascading waterfalls. Dinner that night was supposed to be a dutch at a Chinese restaurant. But they had thought it through, though still forgetting to factor in the tip for the server at such a fancy joint. Collecting money for the pourboire in front of the barista and squabbling over it was both embarrassing and hilarious.

They enjoyed the last night of their trip to the fullest, not wanting it to end, not wanting to go back, not just yet. Later that night, they sat warming themselves in front of a bonfire. It was achingly romantic. The clouds gathered from across the blue mountains, dark and mysterious like the night itself, as if trying to shield them from prying eyes. Mahi leaned on Samar's shoulder, the moody melodies making her heart melt—or was it the effect of Samar's arms, enveloping her like no one was watching?

Ishiqa

High School
Mid-1990s

Ish could not make up her mind about Poorvi. Barring the first day where they had crossed swords, she had been nothing but friendly and sweet. Sucre-sweet to be true. And Ish was wary of her cutesy, mawkish feelers. Ish was a little too aware of the effort Poorvi was trying to put in, her usually pugnacious attitude was nowhere to be seen. It all seemed like a pretence, a sham, put on for the benefit of all, especially Mayank.

But Ish was ready to try her. She wanted an in, and without Poorvi on her side, she didn't stand a chance. Poorvi would make sure of that, Ish had an inkling. Ishiqa, therefore, was eager to gain Poorvi's approval and ignore these undercurrents.

Ish and Poorvi were BFFs, the new baes. Ish would not dare to try on a new dress without a nod from Poorvi. 'Mayank hates red,' Poorvi would stress and Ish would meekly accept. She was buckling under the pressure Poorvi exerted.

My Suitcase Heart

Ish wasn't the trepid, timorous girl she was fast turning into. But love does that to you. It mellows you out, takes away the boom from your bang, and it leaves you with longing and justification. Love does pull a number on you. It is like a schizophrenic attack—your personality takes a complete turn and you don't recognize yourself and you couldn't care less. Ish was in Love.

Poorvi was in Love.

They both were in love and with the same guy.

Poorvi was also at war. And she didn't understand defeat.

'Mayank would never like this dress!' Poorvi explained. 'You look like a lost puppy with that mop of hair on your head.' 'You seem to have put on weight' …

There were more ways than one that Poorvi could use to get under Ish's skin. Ish was now second-guessing herself at every point, unsure of herself, doubting and questioning everything about herself, tired of trying to be on fleek. She was no longer the affable, happy-go-lucky girl who oozed charm. Her smile no longer radiated through her eyes. She was slowly withdrawing in a shell of self-inflicted misery. She was being swallowed into the vortex of conflicting emotions taking her down.

Mayank, meanwhile, was doped up on love. He was oblivious to the ripples that were gaining strength with each passing moment. Mayank had a pinata made especially for Poorvi's birthday as always. Poorvi wouldn't stop gushing about it—how Mayank made such a hullabaloo about her birthday every single time, how he never forgot to bring her favourite flowers and how they would always end up sharing a coffee and stories on her terrace gazebo after everyone at the party had left. Ish suddenly felt like a stranger in their lives. Was Poorvi giving her a subtle hint that Ish should also leave after the party like everyone else? She was not sure any more and Mayank wasn't helping. How could he, he was clueless, blissfully oblivious to what was brewing beneath the surface. He had no inkling that his best friend and his girlfriend were at war. He could never have guessed the diabolic designs and nasty schemes that Poorvi had resorted to.

Poorvi was playing her game well, dealing sugar-coated blows to the yet raw relationship. She was targeting their insecurities and carving a meticulous divide.

The other day, Ish saw Mayank giving Poorvi a chocolate. Later that evening, Poorvi talked to her about it while slurping on that very chocolate. 'Oh this? Mayank gave this to me,' she added coyly, as if on cue.

Ish never got the chocolate or the letter that Mayank sent through Poorvi for her. Nor did she ever get those gifts meant to surprise her. Poorvi made sure of that. Mayank never doubted her. 'She doesn't like childish advances,' Mayank concluded when he noticed Ish's lack of excitement at his little gestures.

Only if he had known better.

Poorvi & Mayank

High School
Mid-1990s

Poorvi did well to hide her bitterness. She thought it best to tread lightly, manoeuvre her way with altered (read: camouflaged) emotions. Poorvi was Ish's new best friend, and Mayank was the happiest. Now his best friend and his love were getting along perfectly. He could now bare his heart to Poorvi and seek her advice. Poorvi knew best and now she was Ish's bae, her girl.

Poorvi was not Ish's girl. Poorvi was Mayank's girl. She was the one who taught Mayank the C3/C4 cycles, the one who laughed at his lame jokes, who talked to him through the night when he was feeling low, she was the one Mayank shared his secrets with, the one Mayank winked at … until Ish arrived. But now, all Mayank could do was talk about Ish, ask after Ish, make notes for Ish, laugh with Ish and wink at Ish! And their shared whispers and secret glances

Poorvi & Mayank

were noticed.

Poorvi was like a shadow now, the extra in a relationship.

Poorvi was not Ish's girl, Poorvi was Mayank's girl and she would make him realize that. Soon! 'Beware the whimsy of fate,' a dark voice tried to warn her … but she was determined.

That day, Poorvi missed school and the next day, and the day after. She refused to come on the phone. Mayank felt uneasy and restless. He wasn't used to not seeing or talking to Poorvi for so long. Ish was as clueless as Mayank was, and he had this weird feeling that she was happier without Poorvi around. The fourth evening, he finally rode to her home on his bicycle. She was sitting on the verandah and seemed well at first glance, oblivious to the appurtenances of luxury that surrounded her (she had grown up taking all of this for granted) and when she noticed, she felt that it was her right to overcompensate for her parents' absence. Her dad was always away on business trips, and she hardly remembered anything about her mother. She had been just two years old when her mother had left the family. Since then, her grandma was all she had.

Mayank flung his cycle, walked up to her, his eyebrows raised, silently questioning her absence from school. 'I am leaving school,' Poorvi announced unceremoniously. Mayank's jaw dropped.

'What? Why?' he stammered.

'Because of you—you and Ish,' she said pragmatically. She looked composed, totally in control. 'I cannot go on pretending any longer, I love you, Mayank and it kills me to see you with someone else. It is too much of an ask to see you day in and day out with her.'

Mayank stood there, her words incomprehensible. 'She is my best friend, she has always been my buddy, my go-to person ... she knows that I love Ish, she knows I am deeply, madly, hopelessly in love with Ish. How can she say what she is saying? How can she feel that way? How can she do that to us?' He was so utterly confused. Nothing made sense right now. Poorvi—his dearest friend, someone he had come to take for granted in his life, someone he sought for every little thing, for all great adventures, for all goofy antics—Poorvi was the one he went to. But this ... this was not something he had ever envisaged.

'I hate Ish. I hate her so much,' Poorvi was blabbering now, her cool demeanour out of the window, her eyes red, her lips quivering, her body trembling. Mayank could take this no further, he turned his back and stormed out. He didn't want to share this space with Poorvi any more, he didn't want to see the hatred for Ish writ large across Poorvi's face, he didn't want to think, to imagine, any harm coming to Ish. His cycle still lay on the porch but he didn't come back to get it.

Poorvi returned to school a fortnight later, her hands bandaged. She had cut her palm and written a long letter to Mayank with that blood before slashing her wrists. The letter was now more or less an open secret. The parents were involved. The school authorities were involved. The matter was being hushed up for the benefit of all involved.

Mayank's parents wanted him to stay away from any further nuisance and had become more vigilant about his daily routine, Poorvi's dad had left for another business engagement, her little 'misadventure' had already cost him a couple of important meetings. Ish had abruptly become distant and wasn't communicating with Mayank any more.

She requested that her seat, and then her class section be changed and was granted that shift surprisingly swiftly. Mayank's friends were no longer sure of Mayank's role in all of this—maybe he had led poor Poorvi on? 'He has always been a flirt, how could he be just friends with her, the two were always inseparable, all over each other until the other girl …'

Tongues were wagging and Mayank was silently and constantly scrutinized by his peers. He wasn't angry; he was devastated. Mayank was drowning. He felt guilty that he had never realized the extent of Poorvi's emotions for him. That blood-soaked letter still brought chills, and Poorvi's pale frazzled face made him sadder. He felt desperately alone, all eyes judging him, observing him, monitoring his every move. He lay on his bed at night, Ish's scent still fresh in his memory, that kiss under the trellis still lingered on his lips and yet, Ish was far away from him. She seemed to have moved on. He could hear her exuberant laughter ringing through the corridors as she passed by his classroom. She had made some new friends, close ones too, it seemed. She was flaunting a new pixie cut, and Mayank wasn't sure whether he loved or hated it—not that his opinion mattered any more. Ish looked very put together, and Mayank seemed to be a small and inconsequential chapter, already read and forgotten. Meanwhile, Mayank's heart felt like a sunless garden, pages torn out of him, leaving gaps which would render his story incomplete forever.

He went to meet Poorvi that day.

She held his hand, brought it to her mouth and kissed it gently. He saw the pain in her eyes, a pain that reverberated through his body. He could understand her loneliness for the first time as he bent down to kiss her ... their lips met, she drew him closer, he let out a sigh, their pain became one.

Poorvi sat with Mayank on the first bench, mitosis/meiosis lessons went ahead as usual. All was great again!

Hiya & Zorawar

Canada
2000

While her cousins and their families revelled in speedboat rides across the cerulean Muskoka Lake, Hiya usually sauntered off to the forest of Screaming Heads. It was her secret haven. Here her demons would leave her body and she could battle it out with them. She spent hours sitting in the wild thicket, staring at the weird stone heads, thinking of nothing. She felt at peace here, amidst the craziness and the quiet.

She would see him almost every other weekend. He brought along a relative or the other to visit this hidden treasure. 'He had way too many relatives,' she mused. They had often exchanged pleasantries—a wave, a smile, a hello-ji—mostly coming from him. Hiya always nodded in forced acknowledgement.

Zorawar was there again that day. Hiya almost resented her secret place being trespassed so very often. He stayed back while his bunch wandered ahead to peek at the artist's abode and the other eccentric sculptures he was still working on.

She stiffened as she realized he was stealthily approaching her. She wanted to flee but she was petrified. He had his fingers on his lips. Now she could see him lunging towards her, his arms ready to grab her. She let out a scream, a loud wild scream before she rolled over into the wild growth surrounding her. She passed out just as it withdrew its fangs from her foot.

She found herself on a hospital bed when she opened her eyes.

Zorawar was there. He winked at her. 'You fainted from fear and not because of the snake venom,' he mocked. She managed a faint smile.

He did not know her story, but he knew fear when he saw it. He had seen Hiya's face turn pale and her body go rigid; Hiya had not seen the snake beside her. She had seen him. She was afraid of him ... but why?

Zorawar and Hiya now met often. He wouldn't yet dare call those dates as she always had a single coffee at his petrol pump's Tim Horton. He could see that she still had her guard up—the accidental brush of his hand was enough to make her twitchy and nervous.

He was patient, and slowly, Hiya had started to open up ...

She needed to let it out, she needed him to know. He might not want to be with her once the skeletons of her past came tumbling out but she wanted to take her chances. She

Hiya & Zorawar

no longer wanted to slash her wrists and see them bleed, to see the pain dripping, drop by drop, out of her body and falling to the ground.

It was not easy for Zorawar to hear it, to see her still cringing in pain and disgust as she recounted the horrors she had lived through. Hiya's mind kept wandering off to dark corners and Zorawar had to keep bringing her back from the damaging alleys of her childhood. It was not easy to know that the person with whom you had fallen in love was carrying a grief so huge, a past so painful that it threatened to haunt the future, to realize that he would have to pick up the pieces until she no longer felt broken …

He was willing to spend a lifetime doing that.

Hiya

High School
Mid-1990s

They were a family of four—'plus one'. Her mother's unmarried brother lived with them as the plus one. The satan was the plus one.

Hiya was blossoming into a young woman, her body now acquiring a luscious fullness. He could now see the rise and fall of her tender body as she sat infront of him, the tightness in his crotch almost as visible as her peaks that pushed against the thin fabric of her white shirt. He had to be patient, he could not risk being caught. How much he wanted to grab her, squeeze the hell out of those round firm balls of flesh till she screamed in agony and ecstasy, to trample her youth beneath him till she begged for mercy.

She dared him every day.

But he had to be patient, wait for an opportune moment for her to be more ready, more ripe. He would pluck her soon,

Hiya

plough her deep. He could feel the wetness around his groin as he excused himself from the table. He would take her on this very table, he could see her splashed naked, ready for him to dive in. He hurried out of the door and went straight into the restroom to relieve himself.

Hiya hated it when he planted moist kisses on her cheeks, and sometimes, when they were on her lips. But she knew her mom would be very angry if she didn't complete her homework in time. He helped her with her homework. He would hoist her up in his lap while she tried solving those sums. He would grope Hiya in the dark corners of the house when no one was watching. He would lift her dress and touch her in places she didn't like. He would always say, 'Touch this, it is a toy.' He would point towards his lower torso. 'We will soon have a play-date,' he would hiss a promise when her mom was not around.

She tried telling her mom but she didn't know how to articulate the words. Once she summoned all the courage and blurted it out to a family friend—'Aunty, my uncle is not good, he is very sexy.' Tears rolled down her eyes, her whole body was trembling but the older lady just sat there, laughing.

'Sexy? So that's a good thing.' She brushed aside the whole thing like a confession from a besotted little girl at puberty. This aunt of hers was a regular at the house, a little in awe of the uncle, now that you come to think of it. The aunt told him what Hiya had said. Hiya got a spanking on her naked butt, unable to even scream because his mouth was on her mouth; violent, hard, shutting it into silence.

She had learnt to live in silence, nobody was willing to listen.

That day, her parents went out for a movie. It was not often that they ventured out together for such a long duration. Hiya tried to be clever and called two of her friends over to keep her company (to keep her safe!). Her uncle surprisingly didn't seem to mind this at all. Little did she know that he saw two more preys to devour. Mahi and Ahana were in the room as he walked in. He was shirtless and had some candies and chewing gum in his fist. He offered it to the trio. He took his hand away as Mahi walked up to him to take one.

'You can have it, but you will have to make a bubble as large as this,' he circled her breast as he said this. She flinched but stood rooted to the spot. He gave all of them those pink gums which they chewed, frozen to the ground. They wanted to flee but instead blew bubbles and he measured each bubble and then their breasts and then kissed the bubble to flatten it and then kissed their breasts. 'See, they are still bigger,' he would say, squeezing. The ordeal went on till Mahi's mom came to pickup the two girls. Hiya's parents too returned almost at the same time. Mercifully, Hiya went to bed soon. She was afraid to sleep but even more afraid to stay awake.

She woke up to the noises from the living room. People were shouting at each other. She rushed downstairs to find Mahi's and Ahana's parents, their voices loud, fury writ large on their faces. Hiya's dad was sitting in a corner, almost sloshed on the sofa, his head between his hands. Her mom stood there in denial—but the ugly secret was out, whether she understood it or not, believed it or not—her brother was a paedophile. He had been molesting her daughter right under their noses, and now, he was hunting for soft prey outside his territory too.

Her dad never recovered from the stroke. Her mom never came out of her denial. Hiya's grandparents packed all of them off to Canada, away from the scandal, away from the prying eyes of suspecting neighbours, away from more misery. Distant relatives took them in and they slowly started to build their life back again. Hiya kept in touch with her friends—they had saved her from doom and from hell. She had scars but had survived. She had lived on to meet this beautiful, sweet, strong, compassionate boy. 'Zorawar' (she liked how his name sounded in her head). She had lived on to love and be loved.

Samar & Mahi

High School
Mid-1990s

Samar had given up on his dreams of becoming an engineer.

'You are the first one I am sharing this with,' he was screaming with joy over the phone, the newspaper with his results clenched tightly in his hand. His roll number was right there, right on the seventh page, right among the other successful candidates. He was going to Nasik. Samar could not wait to celebrate his success with Mahi.

'Congrats!' Mahi said in a high-pitched voice, tears rolling down her cheeks.

Her eyes were swollen and red when Samar met her that evening. 'You have been crying.' He was befuddled. 'Aren't you happy?' He gave her a disconcerted look.

'No, no.' Mahi was quick to cut him short. 'I am thrilled for *you*.' Samar could gather how she stressed on the last word. He had completely forgotten that he would be moving to Nasik soon in his euphoria, some thousand miles away from the love of his life. He had completely forgotten that he himself had predicted that all long-distance relationships were doomed.

His shoulders sagged. He could feel the energy suddenly dissipating from his body. His mind was foggy. All he could register was Mahi standing in front of him, sobbing inconsolably.

Mahi didn't want to cry and show him how vulnerable she felt. She wasn't this needy girl! She didn't want to be an impediment to Samar's success. But neither did she want Samar to go, she couldn't let him go, she was so afraid of losing him, afraid of the thought of being torn apart. She didn't understand how and when Samar had come to mean so much to her, when had she turned so weak and so clingy. She didn't want to understand, all she wanted at this moment was for Samar to stay, to not go, to be with her forever.

'Don't go,' Mahi let out the words, the urgency and the force stunning her as well. Samar looked at her for what seemed like eternity, and finally, he said, 'Okay.'

Just like that.

Mahi looked back, surprised, eyes wide in astonishment. She wasn't expecting this answer. She had expected heated arguments, a complete rejection of her stupid and selfish idea. She was mentally gearing up for endless dark nights with wet pillows, STD phone calls that slowly tapered off in duration and frequency and the slow death of her relationship with Samar.

My Suitcase Heart

'Okay, I won't go,' Samar repeated with a lot more conviction and determination in his voice this time. 'I will talk to my parents today and convince them that I've had a change of heart.' He was now thinking of the task ahead. His parents had always supported him and had never interfered in his choices. This time it would be different though, no one in their sane mind would accept this bizarre irresponsible decision of his. But his mind was made up and he was ready for a showdown in case of one. He was not going. He could not go. He could not imagine being away from Mahi, not seeing her every day, not holding her hands, not sharing that pizza slice or watching her roll her long hair into a messy bun. Some day, looking back, it may seem like a naïve and impulsive decision, which none would support or endorse, but it seemed so right. All is fair in love, after all, and it is not every day that true love comes knocking at your heart. Samar believed in love, he believed in making this one—'his ever after'. He didn't feel answerable to the ones who had not tasted this bitter, sweet, messy and ethereal feeling called love.

Part 2
DIFFERENT DOORS

Samar & Mahi

College
Delhi, India
Late 1990s

When she laughed, the skies could explode but it was so rare now. Her round face was occupied with honeyed eyes which gave nothing away—no stories of years gone by, of having loved and lost, of struggles and triumphs, of life lived.

Maybe she hadn't lived after all. Maybe she had just survived, sailed from one year to the next, struggling to keep herself afloat. Theirs was a generation of broken hearts and broken people. Mahi could be their poster girl.

'Can you fix that dupatta with a pin, please?' Samar said to Mahi.

He was getting weirder and more possessive of Mahi by the day. He skipped classes just to sit outside her classroom, waiting for her to come out, asking her to bunk lectures. Mahi was dressing differently on the behest of Samar and yet, he was always finding fault with it. He would insist on her taking a stole with dresses, to keep her hair tied in a bun, to not line her eyes with kohl. Samar was becoming a tad overbearing and suffocating. At first, this overpossessive attitude thrilled Mahi. She loved all the attention, the 'only mine' kind of assertiveness. Samar had stayed back for her, given up his dream just to be with her. And now, he was around her like her shadow. She needed to get away from the oppressive weight of Samar. Samar was less of a boyfriend and more of a social policeman.

Samar wondered why Mahi had to diligently attend all the classes; after all he had forsaken and sacrificed just to be with her. He had absolutely zero interest in the course he was pursuing, he was just there to be with Mahi. He was paranoid, he hated it when Mahi let anyone or anything else be more important, he hated it when she went out with her friends or to her relatives' houses. Samar was on a short fuse these days, ready to pick a fight at the slightest provocation, and sometimes, at none. Mahi still shivered when she thought of the time when he punched the lights out of that boy who 'accidentally' brushed against Mahi in the University Special.

Mahi was elated to have won the intercollege debating competition; she rushed straight from the hall to the terrace beyond the library on the third floor, the certificates clenched tightly in her hand. She wanted to show them first to Samar, he would be so proud of her. Samar always waited for her on the terrace.

Today too, he was sitting there, looking glum. 'What took you so long?' He sounded angry.

'I won,' Mahi proudly dangled her two certificates.

'Wow, Congrats Ms Awesome Brains,' he said, his tone acerbic.

'Hey, dial down the sarcasm. Why are you taunting me? I haven't had anything to eat since morning, didn't wait for people to congratulate me and I dashed straight to you to share my moment. And you are talking to me as if I have committed some crime,' Mahi said, confused.

'Ta,' he scoffed. 'I am indebted forever, madame, for your sacrifice and thoughtfulness.'

He was being plain mean.

'Samar, why are you being impossible?' A lump had formed in Mahi's chest, threatening to choke her.

'Because I am tired of playing second fiddle while you attend classes, win trophies, grab attention. I don't want you to go anywhere without me, I want people to be aware that you are my girlfriend. I don't want you to roam about "unbranded".'

She raised her hands and made air quotes around the word 'unbranded!' It was her turn to be agitated. 'I am not your fucking property. Don't make things difficult. I am my own person, Samar. I love you but don't try to kill my individuality. I do not like where this is going.' Mahi was fuming now

'Oh, you don't like where this is going? Really, you stopped me from going where I was supposed to go and now you want to go places, eh? Samar was furious. He lunged and grabbed her certificates and tore them apart before she could react.

He had started to resent all her friends (they were his friends too, if only he would remember that). He would even tell his own sister, Ahana, the one who had played cupid to their love story, to buzz off if she ever accompanied Mahi. 'You are scaring her away.' Ahana tried to reason with him. She tried to warn Samar that he was becoming an obsessive, unbearable, insecure boyfriend that any girl would be wary of. Samar wasn't listening, he scoffed at his sister's 'preaching'. 'Spare me the cultural ramifications,' he would say whenever Ahana broached the subject. Samar was turning into someone he was not.

'You have changed so much.' Mahi looked deep into his eyes, still the same warm brown, but the sparkle was long gone.

'I don't make an inventory of my emotions. I am not the person I was a year back. Live with that,' he almost barked at Mahi.

Mahi was getting increasingly fearful of Samar. She loved him, but now, she avoided meeting him every day. He would snap at little things, he was always critical of her choice of clothes and had started to meddle with her routine, demanding hourly reports of her whereabouts. The blank calls at her house were making her parents suspicious as well. She spent less and less time on the phone, had started skipping college and was finding newer ways to not have to see Samar.

Samar & Mahi

Mahi was drifting apart from Samar. She did feel guilty, it was for her that Samar was here and not at some elite institute, designing and innovating wonderful stuff. But she could no longer suffer. She could no longer go on being with such a demanding, humiliating, controlling monster, someone Samar was metamorphosing into.

Samar

College
Late 1990s
Delhi, India

Standing there at the station, he thought of those kisses, those conversations, how she had talked and he had listened and they had kissed. He remembered it like yesterday, all those moments frozen in time. He had made a playlist of her favourite music, painstakingly selecting, sequencing and recording songs in cassettes over cassettes. She, however, mostly looked forward to listening to his seductive, brooding voice, his introduction to each song. For her it was as though all the lyrics, every word, held a deeper meaning, a significance only they could sense, an emotion only they could catch.

But the songs didn't reach her ears any more, he didn't listen to their music any longer. A deep wedge had been driven between them and suddenly they both had more important things to do, things that grown-ups do. They had to be

Samar

practical, pragmatic, focused and real. He had some adulting to do, they could not afford the music any more. Love was no longer a force to stop him. He was ready to fly and grab the opportunities coming his way, to seize his second chance. He was ready to break the shackles and become unhinged.

He turned, half expecting to see her running towards him, he stretched his arms to envelop her (she belonged there), to squeeze her tight and never let her go, to again inhale the delicious smell of wood apples and peaches that threatened to swamp him every time her hair flew into his face, hoping that she would come and stop him. But there was no one familiar in all those million heads that scurried through the doors of the station. She hadn't come. He didn't stay.

The train chugged towards a deep dark tunnel.

Mayank, Ish & Poorvi

College
Late 1990s
Delhi, India

College was pretty uneventful.

Mayank and Poorvi seemed like a solid couple by now. Aadi and Ahana were going strong. Mahi and Samar had gone their separate ways like many young lovers often do. Hiya had moved to Canada, but she kept in touch with the girls. Ishiqa was getting married to some rich guy in the states. Her wedding invite came as a shock to all concerned. Ahana was furious that Ishq was acting so stupidly, suspecting it was only a rebound, the result of a failed relationship.

Mayank felt as if someone had just pulled his heart out of his chest; the words on the invite were fuzzy and incoherent. His mind was playing tricks.

Poorvi was ecstatic but she did well to hide her relief. She was the one who insisted that everyone attend the wedding. It would also provide her with a chance to rub her relationship with Mayank in Ish's face. She wanted to savour her triumph and celebrate it too.

Ish was resplendent in the red and gold zardozi lehenga. The tikka on her forehead made Mayank's heart skip a beat. He could not bear to look at her, he could not bear to look away. Samar grabbed his arm and ushered him towards the bar. No words were exchanged. 'Another large, please,' said, over and over, and it kept resonating, setting the tone for the rest of the evening.

Ish was married.

Mayank and Poorvi were a solid couple now.

Ishiqa

Circa 2000, New York

The story begins at Quogue, New York, slightly removed from the happening party scenes at the Hamptons, home to Ishiqa from now on.

The new bride was greeted by a deer grazing beside a couple of snow-white rabbits frolicking through the gardens. All images of the glitz of Manhattan that she had dreamt about while flipping through the pages of those glossy magazines had faded to the background; she was completely besotted.

Deer in the yard, cherry blossoms in the background, the daffodils flashing welcoming smiles, bobbing their heads in excitement.

The first evening was spent in getting acquainted with her staff; they seemed welcoming but nervous. Ish soon set out, excited to explore the neighbourhood, to get a hang of the beach which was right at the backdoor. She could see a storm approaching and so, her discovery trail had to be cut

Ishiqa

short and, she finally settled to the pitter-patter against her window. Ranveer was not home, he had taken a separate cab from the airport. Ish was okay about the fact that he was not there to carry her past the door, she had outgrown past the kissing-under-the-mistletoe season.

It had been a week since the wedding: the festivities, endless customs and the packing had taken up most of her time. She hadn't found the time to register that something was amiss, something that didn't seem right. Maybe she was too busy nursing her broken heart and convincing herself that this was meant to be. Ranveer, her new husband, had been missing most of the time; the only conversation they had had was on the wedding night.

'Who was that guy? He couldn't keep his eyes off you,' Ranveer had asked, and while he had tried to put it casually, the sneer was unmistakable. Ish did not make much of it. Ranveer was just trying to break the ice, she concluded.

That night, the sex—it couldn't be called anything more—was a little rough, but then you always discount the first night. Ish could not put a finger on it but something just didn't seem to fit into place. She was trying not to think about anything, she just wanted to move ahead and take each day as it came. Despite her sixth sense warning her, she failed to read into the hints.

There was to be no honeymoon for now and they were flying back to New York as soon as the wedding functions were over.

My Suitcase Heart

She should not have ignored her intuition, she thought. She should have listened to the small voice in her heart that had been telling her to be cautious. The nightmare slowly started to unravel soon after they returned to the States.

On most days, Ranveer was not home, gambling his time and money away in Atlantic City (she learnt of it later). And she was afraid of him when he would finally arrive, stinking of whisky and smoke, climbing atop her to satisfy his carnal desires. She had resisted the first time—smack!—the sting of that slap still seared through her being.

Some nights, he did not come back: no phone call, no text and so, Ish would go off to sleep, anxious that the keys to the house and her bedroom would turn any moment. Ish was not a lily-livered girl, but the shock and suddenness of what life had thrown at her—in a foreign place among strangers—was something she had to learn to deal with. Her life was spiralling out of control and she was yet to figure out how to save herself from being thrown into a deep dark dungeon with no escape.

Then one day, Ranveer barged in with a girl on his arm; she didn't look like one of the girlfriends he had boasted about.

'Ish, come here,' he commanded. They were in the living room, all three of them. Ish waved at the housekeeper; the latter knew when to disappear.

'Look at her, elfin and petite, that's what I like in a woman.' He was fondling the breasts of the woman he had brought in

Ishiqa

while talking to her. Ish turned around, she could not endure the vulgarity. He was now pulling Ish's hair.

'Woman! Watch and learn. You lie like a log when I make love to you. Maybe you are still thinking about that dork who had the hots for you, but let me tell you, it was good riddance for him. You cannot satisfy a man,' he said. All this while, undoing the other woman who was comfortably splashed on the couch, not even blinking an eye. The two seemed to be getting a kick out of her misery.

Ish threw up. Every single cell in her body revolting at the orgy playing out in front of her eyes, but he carried on with his job, and once he was done, he lurched at the stupefied Ish, and with one strong push, banged her head against the wall.

'You can't let me have my moment, woman, can you?' The maniac spoke, unleashed. She could feel the warm blood dripping down her face. Her head hurt like it would explode any moment, but not before she dialled.

911.

Divorce was smooth, although a long-drawn process—the Indian embassy had intervened and Ish was willing to drop the charges in lieu of her freedom. However, she could not get the financial assistance she had hoped for. She soon discovered that Ranveer had actually nothing left in his name—mortgages and gambling debts had eaten up all his wealth. She had decided she would not go back to India and she would build her life from scratch in this country, where destiny had brought her. She refused to go down without a good fight or go back.

Over the years, she had grown tougher, sort of impermeable to emotion; she had built an impenetrable wall around her. She didn't want to hear the echoes from the past, a past full of fear and grief. She enrolled herself into a community college and initially her dad sent some money to take care of her basic needs; apparently, her part-time waitressing was not enough to see her through the first couple of years. Ish was a trooper though, she joined a real estate firm and started off by setting up showcase houses on the market, decorating them, creating themes, weaving a picture of the lifestyle the house could offer if made into a home. Very soon, she acquired a licence as a real estate broker and now had some prestigious listings up her sleeves. She had recently sold a beautiful five-bedroom cottage to the 2017 Mrs India America, and she was so glad that she could find perfect homes for people.

She was, maybe, making up for the lack of her own perfect home.

Ahana & Aadi

Circa 2000, Vevey, Switzerland

Ahana woke up in a sweat. She was afraid to look around at first. Gradually, as the memories of the nightmare grew fainter, she tried to gather her thoughts and calm her nerves.

Deep breaths, in and out, in and out … she focused on her breathing.

It was another of her bad dreams, she had been having so many of them lately. In-between mastering two foreign languages, hustling work and home, while not forgetting to call and check on all her friends, Ahana still found herself alone in a dark corner. It was a sunless tunnel with no escape. She had no grip on her thoughts; her mind wandered, unbridled, into uncharted territories, where gloom was her only companion. She could not share it with anyone. Her loneliness, her anxiety, her battles were hers to deal with.

How alone is actually alone? Feeling alone in a crowded room, in a space filled with your loved ones. When you want to be surrounded, but with emptiness, where your heart wanders to places so dark and deep that your eyes do not see who and what is around.

She could not show her weakness; nobody would understand, she herself didn't. The spells of self-pity and self-loathing came all of a sudden. One minute she was laughing, and the next, boom! she would go tumbling down a bottomless pit. She could blame it on the three miscarriages and a couple of failed IVF procedures, the extreme hormone therapies that she had undergone, but Aadi did not let her think about any of it, and so, she didn't; at least not in front of him.

And so, she found herself in this wretched place, where no one would find her—the deepest, darkest, unplumbed corner of her mind. Ahana was a strong, outgoing, cheerful girl ... depression was a word she refused to acknowledge or accept. She was not going to seek any help.

'Shrinks are for losers,' she had concluded and this very denial was becoming her worst enemy.

The mask was slipping way too often and Aadi was tired of being the multitasker, the balanced one. The words sounded trite and set him up in a cage of stereotypes: what a man should be, how a husband must behave, always in control, in check of his emotions, the family's well-being, their happiness, their house and their household. He was jaded, overwhelmed with the act he had to put up. But he would continue to do this, he promised himself. They could not afford anything less.

Ahana & Aadi

They were the got-it-together couple, the ones that kept the hope alive, kept the faith in the institution of marriage still strong. And he would hold the fort. He would never let go.

Adi was always finding ways and means to keep Ahana happy and excited. He knew that the only way he could keep her from slipping into her dark shell was to keep her motivated and thrilled about something or the other: an event, a movie, a get-together, a shopping trip or some travel plans. Thankfully, he could still afford the whimsies and the splurge, but he also knew how short-lived and temporary such things were. He needed some stability, some permanence and a lot of hope.

He assumed that the trip with their friends would do Ahana some good (she was always so excited about planning and executing events and travel) and maybe then, when she was ready to listen, he would again broach the subject of adoption.

Rachelle

Germany
2000

Samar liked his coffee strong. He walked across the corridor to make a fresh one, himself this time.

Life in Walldorf was nothing to write home about. He came to office every day at 9 a.m., leaving for home at 5 p.m., but was usually spotted hanging by a beer café till late. Walldorf was a quaint German town, idyllic and halcyon, known for cultivating white asparagus. It was better known for the headquarters of the multinational software giant SAP.

How Samar ended up at SAP is a long tale, involving his grit and determination, perseverance, but not without a generous sprinkling of luck. The company ticked all the right boxes for him: the work–life balance (blah blah), the environment that encourages open and free expression of ideas, a foreign land where he could drown in his own sorrows and nobody would even notice. Not that he was complaining.

Rachelle

He had a swanky office, a relaxed schedule (and why on earth would he want that?), a dedicated staff who looked up to him, projects that kept him ticking ...

"You have been stirring that coffee cold." A silvery voice disrupted his thoughts. It was the new girl, the redhead recently promoted to the main building. She didn't quite sound German to him.

'Rachelle.' She extended her hand.

'Samar,' he replied curtly.

'We know that already, Boss,' she quipped. Samar turned a beetroot red; he hated it when someone called him that. He stammered, not knowing what to say or how to wrap up this awkward conversation without sounding condescending or gruff.

Samar usually kept to himself, refraining from indulging in small talk with his co-workers. He knew that his staff called him stiff and starchy. He liked things this way.

Rachelle kept bumping into him on many such coffee jaunts. Samar had started to make his own coffee pretty regularly of late.

'Do you only do coffee?' she asked playfully one day.

'What?' Samar was confused. Rachelle kept throwing him off balance.

'I mean, would you care for some beer tonight?' Rachelle offered. Samar, obviously, had to refuse. He was not looking to spend time with women, not since Mahi.

'Yes, sure,' he had blurted out before he could even think.

'So, it's a date.' Rachelle marched off, beaming, her heels making that clicking sound of victory that reverberated dangerously through the corridors.

It is not a date, Samar tried to reason with himself, it is just two co-workers hanging out for a pint ...

The date was one of the many that followed ... Jaggerbombs soon replaced the beer. How the café one day led them to his bachelor pad still remains a mystery to Samar. The company gifted them a luxury trip to Amsterdam for their honeymoon.

Vivid flowers nodding their dainty little heads as the breeze gently caressed, colours exploding in all their glory, eyes soaking in the sheer expanse and magnificence of nature's bounty. It was a scene straight out of a Bollywood dream sequence.

Planning the entire trip around the blooming period, making sure to catch the bobbing heads of colourful tulips dancing their wild dance was no easy task, but Rachelle had put her mind to it and she would settle for no less. They postponed their honeymoon for April is when you really want to arrive in the Netherlands to soak up all the festivities, all themed around the ephemeral tulips. It is spring everywhere and a thick veil of cherry blossoms and blooms of pristine white on almond trees are an added bonus.

'Welcome to the beautiful canal city of Amsterdam ...'

Meanwhile, Mahi was punching the keys on her laptop like a maniac. She had to submit the piece by tomorrow, and she still hadn't visited Keukenhof—the famous tulip garden

Rachelle

on the outskirts of Amsterdam.

The first day of the honeymoon was spent settling into the plush NH Collection two-bedroom apartment overlooking the main canal. Rachelle wasn't particularly happy with the bland view from the room they were first offered and so an upgrade was arranged.

The apartment is still etched in Samar's memories. The fireplace in the lounge, huge bay windows with a glimpse of the buzz, and how could he forget that couch? It was perfectly placed, you could sit there for hours looking at the canal, becoming a part of that high life of the city and still feel yet alone. How could he forget that couch, fire crackling in the vintage fireplace, music flowing through the open bay windows ... Samar wanted to pick all the flowers from the tulip fields and give them to Mahi ... Mahi!

Their eyes connected at the souvenir shop; his heart skipped a beat. She was approaching. The store was so crowded, he needed some air, and there she was, still as radiant, as beautiful as he remembered.

Once again, Samar was experiencing the brain fog associated forever with young, reckless love. He associated it with Mahi. He wanted to disown the reactions of his body and his mind. He wanted to run from the scene.

'Samar, oh my god, of all places, we meet here!' Mahi was saying something else, he was not listening ...

'Do you two know each other?' Rachelle nudged Samar.

'Umm ... yes! This is Mahi,' and then turning to her.

'Mahi, this is my wife, Rachelle.'

Samar was having trouble forming simple words.

'Ah, Mahi, I have heard so much about you. You are so beautiful.' Rachelle didn't seem perturbed by the fact that Samar's old flame had bumped into them 'accidentally' on their honeymoon. But she was wrong; Rachelle was very wrong to have ignored her feminine instincts. Things were never the same again, the beer never tasted the same, never, even when Kian was born some months later and Samar decorated the entire home (not without some help from Ahana and Aadi) with tulips especially flown in—all those years in SAP had made sure that he could afford this little indulgence. How could things ever be the same?

It was Mahi whose name he called out, by the fireplace, on the couch, when Rachelle and he were together in the throes of ecstasy, his eyes closed, his body trembling over hers but not for her. And she heard it, loud and clear above the music that flowed in from down the canal.

The apologies were meaningless. Of course, she would forgive him, but how could she forget?

Samar

Germany
2000

The room looked bare and forlorn, emptied of all its accoutrements. His son was inconsolable in his arms, though still too young to understand what was lost.

Kian was sensitive enough to know that something was terribly wrong—Mamma was not there to make it all right; she would not have let him cry for so long, she would have scolded Papa for troubling Kian ... why was she not coming to hold him? He missed her warm scent so much.

Samar, however, was entirely focused on the card he held between his fingers.

> Sorry for Your Loss
> Love,
> Mahi

The world outside the window did not slacken its pace, not

even for a second as Samar's came to a standstill.

A head-on collision with a speeding van, he was told. For a week she was tethered to a ventilator, and he was tethered to a hope. Sandcastles and hopes are eventually swamped by raging tides. He felt nothing except for a surging pain, looming, waiting to become a giant sea swell and take him away from the shore once again.

The first few months after she died were a blur spent in mourning, with grief manifesting in every possible way. He was unable to eat, to drink, to walk across the street without her loss following him. He would frequently scroll through their texts on his phone, remembering how she once teased him, recalling their many conversations, the moments they had shared ... trying to make sense of a life that no longer included her. He would read and reread those conversations, as if rummaging through an overcrowded drawer for something lost.

Rachelle was gone, just like that.

She had taken revenge for his one mistake, in that one moment. But hadn't she said that she had forgotten all of it? he thought.

They had been happy, he made sure they were. They went on picnics together and they laughed and they drank beer.

But she was gone.

Mahi

2000

Mahi was someone who loved rose wine. She liked the wine not because it tasted good but because she was in love with the colour of that sparkling liquid. She often wanted a car just because the shape of the backlight attracted her. She was like a child in this way—moody, impulsive, whimsical and illogical. It was difficult to understand her and almost impossible to cope with her. Samar was her anchor, indulging her, yet keeping her grounded. Without him, she was lost.

She had been trying hard to fill the void he had left. She tried not to think about what was and what could have been, to not blame herself for Samar walking out on them. Her heart still pined for Samar. She still didn't quite understand what she could have done differently. She still kept track of Samar through Ahana (who more than obliged) and she filled in the details from time to time.

Mahi had dabbled in many things after college, but none

of them made her heart sing; she always found an excuse to leave. Her solo trip to Bali was a turning point though, and it brought some meaning to her seemingly directionless life. Nights in Bali were blissfully serene and the days were unhurried, spent watching the waves roll while sipping iced mojitos. She did go parasailing and the wind was unfortunately very strong that day. She was undeterred by the resilient weather, but she had a tough time finding a beach centre still offering the service. Taking a glass-bottomed boat to Turtle Island and the donut ride also seemed tempting, but she had other things on her mind—a trip to the happening Kuta beach topping the charts. Bali turned out to be a trekker's paradise. Bucolic vistas of terraced rice fields spread out before her, while dramatic volcanoes loomed in the backdrop and waterfalls spilled out of luxuriant hills. She was spoilt for choice by this bounty of nature, the thriving cultural scene and the legendary nightlife all rolled into this one glorious island. But what she remembered Bali most for was its riotous frangipani, for the boisterous locals, for the thriving tribal markets, for the interesting palette of colours that curated a fresh art gallery each day as the sun began to set beyond the clear sky and cerulean sea, for a thousand different suns.

She seemed to have finally found her calling in travel. Being a traveller came with its perks: history lessons over the weekends, time travel to exotic worlds, capturing mystical stories of faraway places. Being in a strange land helped her do away with her inhibitions; she could be alone, be in a

Mahi

crowd, be wild, dance with abandon, touch, feel, push the envelope, be spontaneous, feel alive and just be herself, even if temporarily.

'Travel is like love … a forever kind of love,' she once wrote and the post had gone viral, garnering thousands of likes. She, however, abstained from participating in the Traveller vs Tourist debate that hounded all those who were even the slightest bit interested in travelling. Who was she to judge? As someone who loved to go to exotic destinations but had a (bottomless) bucket list of all the touristy ones too, she was cautious to not become smug like the many influencers around her. She did not quite understand the need to define travel or the wanderlust that evolved around it. She would love to luxe it out on her holidays if she could afford to, and at the same time she admired those taking a solo backpacking trip to seek the stars and the sky. She travelled because she found comfort in her sojourns; travel had reignited that spark in her: to explore, to dream, to live. She liked visiting different countries, experiencing their culture, their food and the innumerable vistas.

The joy of unravelling hidden treasures made her forget about her loneliness, even if it was for a short while. Often, she would wake up in the middle of the night, on a strange bed in a foreign country, nowhere she knew, nowhere she belonged to … there was no one she knew, no one she belonged to. She was alone and falling, plummeting into the dark. The next morning, she would book a flight to a more exotic destination, drinking kombucha tea, tasting hot tamales, slurping handcrafted gelatos, looking at honey-dipped houses and gazing endlessly at emerald shorelines.

She had started to derive a strange pleasure in moving towards the unknown. Her travel articles were now a regular feature with some reputed magazines and she grew popular for writing about hidden gems and unexplored places. She still remembered how excited she was when her first write-up was featured in print! She was jumping with joy when she called her mom and Ahana. She slowly graduated to travel photography as her microblogs demanded pictures to define the places she described. She revelled in her new-found popularity as a travel blogger with millions of followers. Though she refused to acknowledge that all her travels were a quest, offering a sliver of hope and a journey to find a way back to the life she once had, to find a cocoon where her heart could finally rest.

Mahi

Mahi
Circa 2000

Paris was like a bucket of ice hurled at her.

It came as a sharp and painful reminder that travel was just Mahi's way of running away from her actual feelings. She could never get over Samar. Her heart throbbed for what seemed like a distant dream. Samar had remained just that, distant. She tried to reach out to him a couple of times after Rachelle's demise, but Samar did not seem interested in reforging a bond.

Who could tell that he was busy battling his own demons? How could he forgive himself for what he had done to the two women who had ever mattered to him? How could he move ahead with his life when guilt bogged him down? They—him and Mahi—the ones that were once meant to be, had absolutely no future together. The past had corrupted it all. He had let it all go; he was the villain of his own story. He could not let himself dream. Never again, he did not deserve it. He had nothing to offer to anyone any more, he had been emptied of all emotions.

A familiar lassitude overpowered Mahi soon after she boarded the flight to Paris. She wanted to flee, but her legs would not listen and she remained glued to the seat. She had realized her mistake, but it was too late. No, she wasn't ready. Paris was too soon in her scheme of things; her wounds were still fresh, her heart still tender.

Paris was Mahi and Samar's dream. They had talked about it so often, imagined watching the Eiffel Tower light up and dazzle them both. She swore that she could imagine the taste of the macarons at Laduree, which they had wanted to share while sifting through glossy travel magazines. They would have walked the streets of Montmartre, retracing the footsteps of artists like Vincent Van Gogh and Pablo Picasso. They had daydreamed about walking hand in hand, kissing, giggling, feeling happy. But here she was, covering the Annual Boulangerie Fair at the Parc des Expositions. She deliberately gave Laduree a miss and went to have a hot chocolate at Angelina, not that anybody could complain about the heavenly drink there either, but her heart was not in it.

She sat there, staring at her cup—the drink tasted bitter and muddy, the skies seemed grey and gloomy. She noticed the blooming wisterias and snapdragons, the tubs of pink damask roses against the lavish lattice work, but her mind wandered elsewhere. How the two of them had debated

Mahi

over Moulin Rouge, whether cabaret was a cultural heritage and whether it needed to be preserved or was it high time that such a sexist form of entertainment be canned and condemned. Mahi now realized how differently the two of them thought. Samar could have spent hours marvelling at the collections the Louvre housed, while she would have easily picked Versailles and Monet's Garden to spend the day in front of. He bent more towards the artsy, while she was all for the vibe and the web of tales around a place. He loved to visit a place to admire its architectural details while she loved to indulge in the history and knew about it from the books they chose to read, the local tourist spots they chanced to visit back home, the conversations they had. They were poles apart, an imperfect fit, a contrast of sorts and yet they had dreamt of places and moments and a life together. Love is not about perfect matches but about exotic blends that come together to create magic.

The more Mahi thought of Samar, the more she felt lost.

The city of love, the city of light, this wonderland. Its sparkle and its effervescence had started to make her miserable, and the sight of lovey-dovey couples was making her more and more aware of the void in her heart. She was fighting hard to hold back her tears as she strolled along the Seine, alone and lonely.

She had brought this on herself. If only she had not pushed Samar away, or if she had let go in the first place ... for the first time she found herself regretting her decisions, her choices, her impulsiveness. She could not turn back the clock, undo what had been done.

A small resilient voice in her head told her that she could not have done things any differently. She should not have had to make the hard choice between love and self-respect. Shouldn't she reconcile with her destiny and move on?

Mahi was her best counsel in times like these. She took a deep breath and ventured on to buy tickets to a cruise down the river; she intended to dance her heart out that night.

'But before that, I shall indulge in some retail therapy at the Champs-Elysées,' Mahi decided.

Part 3
THE REUNION

The Sailing

2020

Crafting a perfect itinerary was the toughest part of Ahana's plan—what with so many islands to choose from and so many places to visit, all within a limited number of days. And then, Ahana discovered the perfect vacation plan: an eleven-day-long cruise covering seven beautiful islands of Greece. It was more or less everything they wanted out of this tour served to them on a platter. There would be no fuss while planning for transportation, of lugging the baggage from place to place, no worries about the language barrier. It would just be a pure, unadulterated voyage.

The port of embarkation was Venice in Italy. But who was complaining?

'Happy is the man, I thought, who before dying has the good fortune to sail the Aegean Sea,' said Nikos Kazantzakis in Zorba the Greek and Ahana's happiness knew no bounds. After an initial reluctant attitude, Samar for once was equally involved in finalizing the details. It turned out that he had recently developed an on-board communication app, Drifty, for one of the big cruise liners and the company was happy to offer him a very good deal.

Travel day is always a bit of a slog, even though people write odes about the journey being the reward. But this time, the experience broke all past records of their tortuous misadventures. A few days before their journey was to begin, there was news of Jet Airways being in some kind of trouble and many domestic flights were being delayed endlessly, or worse, cancelled.

However, Mahi's panic button was not pushed until the effect started to show up on the international routes as well. Thankfully, her booking was through KLM, which had a code-share agreement with the airway company for an India-to-France connection and thereafter, she was flying to Venice with Air France. She did write to KLM to ask if she needed to worry about the situation with the situation getting grim day by day as more and more flights were being grounded and the financial mess seemed to be getting murkier.

KLM sent her the usual standard reply for the mails and after her sundry tweets, thereafter, they explained that they were closely monitoring the situation and that, as of now, they had no knowledge of any change in the said flight schedule. Jet Airways, though, was claiming to refund the tickets that had already been issued. But it was hard to get hold of anyone in the authorized staff to give them a clear picture.

The Sailing

A day before she was to fly, Mahi got an email from KLM that her flight had been cancelled due to unforeseen circumstances and that she would either be placed on the waiting list for those who wished to be accommodated in another flight or she could claim a full refund and be compensated for the inconvenience caused. 'As you understand, these are trying times and we regret that your plans have been jeopardized. We again regret the inconvenience,' the email read.

Mahi was in despair; she did not want a refund and she could not afford to be on the wait list or she would miss the cruise. Her itinerary did not allow her that kind of freedom, and she was busy! She tried to marshal her thoughts. Moping about the helplessness of the situation wouldn't help, neither would her being angry, she decided and picked up the phone to ring the airlines. The line was busy; she tried again and again and then some more. She had nothing better to do at the moment and her persistence paid off. The staff seemed apologetic and eager to help; the man on the line tried to patiently listen as Mahi rambled on and on … about how she could not afford to not go and that any amount of compensation would not help … an entire fortnight had already been paid for and it included a non-cancellable cruise.

Mahi also dropped a hint: she had a humongous following on her blog, after all. She normally did not take undue advantage of this fact, but these were exceptional times and she was desperate. The employee on the other end turned out to be quite efficient after that. The man worked out a new flight schedule with Turkish Airways, and it seemed most suitable to Mahi. She would, of course, have to spend over seven hours at Istanbul airport but she would not lose a day and would be in time to catch the cruise. She heaved a sigh of relief when the confirmation email of her revised flight schedule arrived.

However, her ordeal was yet to begin.

Turkish Airlines was apparently overbooked and they were in no mood to honour the KLM-issued flights. They were already cancelling some of their own reservations. The KLM customer care at the airport took forever to respond and when they did, they had nothing to offer but a rescheduling of tickets and an apology. But Mahi was not giving up without a fight; she used all the tools at hand: pleading, threats of suing, ultimately realizing that patience was the only virtue which was going to pay off. Luckily for her, the flight had been delayed and she still had time to keep trying. By now, the ground staff had softened towards her upon seeing her determination and sensing her urgency. One of them dropped a hint that if she waited long enough without being too conspicuous and vocal, then maybe she would have a chance once all Turkish Airways members were accommodated. The other KLM members who had been rescheduled like her had given up hope and were soon leaving one by one.

She sat through the whole tiresome process, anxiety and panic on two ends of a see-saw in her mind. Finally, ten minutes before boarding, her name was called and she

The Sailing

was ushered in for security checks with the promise that her luggage would follow. Once on the plane and after gulping down an iced glass of water, she was able to think straight again.

The friends all had stories to share when they finally met at the check-in counter of the cruise, whacked and looking worn down from the journey and the years between them. It took a while to recognize each other and get into the groove.

The ship set sail, not long after they had freshened up, and they were soon directed towards the dock for a mandatory fire drill.

Their first stop in Greece was Corfu, a picturesque island floating between Italy and the west coast of mainland Greece on the Ionian Sea. It boasted of lush olive and pistachio groves, mountains and woodlands, the deep cerulean hues of the crystal-clear sea and cliff-backed pink golden beaches. Corfu is rumoured to be the setting of many famed novels, a muse of writers and the perfect canvas to sundry acclaimed stories—Shakespeare's *Tempest* figuring in the list. The old Corfu town is replete with elegant venetian architecture and some very fine museums. The ruins of the fort make for a stunning backdrop. The group, meanwhile, seemed more interested in the hustle-bustle of the noisy and boisterous agora or marketplace. Later, when the girls were alone, and because the boys could not keep in step with their shopping spree, a gossip girl episode was unleashed.

Poorvi was left behind with the unsuspecting Hiya.

'She looks at me as if my hot bod is melting all the glaciers,' Ish fumed.

'And her icy stares will restore equilibrium,' Ahana quipped. Poorvi had ruffled quite a few feathers with her critical and snarky attitude and the gang was fast losing their patience.

'Overbearing bitch. I would literally have taped up her mouth if she had gone on with her train-bragging bit any longer. Who does she think she is—an avatar of Greta Thunberg?'

Ahana shushed Ish as familiar voices approached them.

Poorvi had been making a show of her concern for the environment, throwing around terms like 'flight shaming', 'carbon footprint' and 'global warming' in every sentence. However, she didn't seem to be walking the talk. How could she ever explain this whistle-stop cruise vacation of hers if she felt so strongly about the cause? Her words sounded so empty and hollow. She seemed full of herself—an elitist prick. But then she had always been like this, they thought. Mayank was the sole reason that she was still a part of the gang.

Mayank

Cruise ship
2020

He drained the last of his beer while contemplating opening another pint. Ishiqa was sprawled on one end of the sofa near him, her slender frame occupying only a little of the wine-hued velvet.

Something stirred inside him.

He wanted nothing more than to fill that empty space beside her … he yearned to lie next to her, to let her familiar scent envelop him and to find her fingers caressing his hair like one would stroke a pet.

Mayank studied his friends for a moment—Zorawar didn't know much, but Aadi and Samar were his go-to people. Did they know … did they have an inkling of what was brewing in him? Would they understand? Nothing in their demeanour suggested it. And yet, the winks, the nudge at the elbow, their devilish smiles hinted otherwise. They would never tell him to stop, it was not their place to advise. They would not tell him the right from the wrong, and it was his choice to make. Aadi and Samar had never interfered, judged or tried to give unsolicited advice. But he knew that they had never approved of Poorvi, or about how his relationship with Poorvi had panned out. They accepted it ... but not without their reservations.

It was Mayank they rooted for, and if he was happy, well, they were ready to tolerate Poorvi's hysterics.

Mayank & Ishiqa

Cruise ship
2020

'Ish—iqa!' Mayank called, almost forgetting that Poorvi was watching his every move. His heart shifted gears recklessly, and a crackle of electricity went up his spine every time Ish so much as looked at him. 'Ishiqa, you are coming for the Captain's Party tonight, na?' Mayank tried to tone down the excitement in his voice.

'Yup,' she answered nonchalantly. She was quite excited about the 'dress up' event but did well to keep it to herself. She hadn't mentioned her bespoke sequined bodycon to someone, had she? Ahana did catch her smize (smile through the eyes, for the uninitiated) and nudged her. 'Why are you being all hoity-toity around Mayank, Ish?' Ahana probed.

'Well, the act is more for Poorvi's benefit,' Ish was gloating now.

'Stay away from trouble, will you,' Ahana beseeched.

My Suitcase Heart

Ish answered with a wink.

At night, that night, Ish came down oozing sex (appeal). Her long mane swept back, a dainty clip holding back any rogue strands, her body one with that shimmery veil of a dress. Gold was his favourite colour, Mayank concluded in this moment. Her face was angelic despite the pout that she had perfected. Her hips swayed delicately as she flitted down one step to another, lighting up the entire staircase. Mayank could watch her walk up to him like that for all eternity, slowly undoing her with his eyes alone.

'You look tramazing, Ish.' Poorvi hugged her awkwardly. She smelt of wood apple and forest trails; Poorvi was now very aware of herself. She had felt a huge headache coming on and had chosen to just throw a purple cashmere sweater over the only jeans she had brought. 'Travel light.' Her motto laughed in her face.

'Drop the gape,' Hiya whispered to Mayank, half afraid that Poorvi would have noticed how besotted her husband was with Ishiqa by now. Ishiqa, meanwhile, was in no mood to hold back that day ... but then, when did she ever? Her rocky marriage and an early divorce had made her stronger than ever. Her gay abandon, uninhibited lifestyle and no-strict-rules policy was the talk of Quogue, the small hamlet where she now lived in the US of A. She wasn't bothered by gossip; people only talked, they talked when her husband used to hit her black and blue, they talked when she filed for a divorce and refused to go back to her 'home', they talked and did nothing else. Tonight, she would think nothing of it.

Mahi and Ahana shared troubled glances while Ishiqa held up her third drink and said, 'Bottoms up!' Their conversations flowed over generous helpings of bruschetta, corn fritters and creamy jacket potatoes. They were reminiscing about the halcyon days, their antics as the inseparable gang, their nights out, their scandals and their heartbreaks. Mahi shot a furtive glance towards Samar, trying to gauge his reaction when they brought up topics that bothered her, memories that haunted her. 'Nothing there,' she concluded. He had turned into an island. Remote and cut off ...

Each time he needed another drink, Zorawar would ask and constantly refill everyone else's glasses too, yet always he was a glass or two ahead. He would insist on a new cocktail mix he had recently chanced upon or a classic, to stay in the mood. He was a people-pleaser, humouring the guys, complimenting the women and never letting the booze or the conversation stop. He was slowly making room into the coveted group, for he knew Hiya would love it if he was accepted with open arms.

Hiya, on the other hand, was happy just being there. She had mastered the art of being a wallflower. With her phone out of network range, Kindle was what she found solace in. It was her way to escape the real world.

Samar, meanwhile, was doing well to act oblivious when some of the anecdotes inched closer home. He knew how damaging it could prove to be if he went down memory lane, opening up old wounds again, vignettes of their story ready to burst at the seams and lie exposed. Samar continued to sip on his mojito like he couldn't care less; his participation was limited, like a spectator sitting on the fence, more interested in the popcorn on the stands than the game. Samar did well to hide, to hide himself from the onslaught of raw emotions and buried memories.

Aadi called Ahana to the dance floor as their favourite number played. Poorvi was having quite a struggle sitting there as her headache grew stronger. The loud music, the cacophony of clinking glasses and the laughter was not helping her cause. But she would endure the whole damn thing even if it killed her, she would guard what was hers, she would keep Mayank away from that wretched Ishiqa. The headache, however, got the better of her and finally she caved in as it grew unbearable.

She shot a glance at Mayank. He was with Zorawar, deep in conversation about some mundane thing it seemed. 'Hmm, in safe hands,' she thought. She went up to Hiya, 'I will take a rain check. Keep an eye on these two.' She pointed towards Zorawar and Mayank. Hiya understood what she actually meant. They all knew that Mayank had carried a torch for Ishiqa all these years; and a small spark would be enough to reignite the flame. Poorvi excused herself. The torture was unbearable now, maybe she would pop a pill, rest for a while and come back again.

'The party is still young,' she smirked as she left.

The dance floor was on fire. Ishiqa gestured to Mayank

to join her as Sikkidim began to play. How they had moved to that song once.

Their bodies were perfectly in sync, the rhythm building as they swayed in each other's arms. He was ridiculously hot, Ish thought, his eyes were black like the night and dangerously deep; it was almost unbelievable that a person could be so attractive and yet so unaware of it. She lifted her mouth, he bent a little ... the kiss seemed to last forever. She was now standing on her toes to match his urgency. The air around them was thick and volatile. The dervish dance wilder as their hips touched, and he bit her tongue.

She opened her eyes. They were here, in Greece, and he was married.

She pulled back. Flirting was one thing, she liked to ruffle some feathers, but this ...

Mayank's voice had turned raspy. 'Ishq?' He gave her a quizzical look, still swooning from the warm rush that had taken over his body. Ish could see the naked hunger in his eyes, the three cocktails and a couple of tequila shots did nothing to help her either. 'Mahi and Ahana are looking,' was all she could come up with. But no one was actually watching, they had thought it better to give the two some privacy soon after things had started heating up.

'Let's get some fresh air.' Mayank was leading her towards the deck. Ish did not resist.

Out on the deck, Mayank did not stop, he increased his pace, grabbing her arm and leading her through another door.

Her arm hurt but she wasn't complaining.

'Where are we going?' she asked. They were walking on thin ice.

'To your room,' he replied, and she was okay with that. She knew what going to the room meant. She longed for it. They scrambled through the corridors like two addicts rushing in search of a drag. The lift took forever to reach the seventh floor.

Ishiqa fumbled with her keys. Mayank was all over her, each passing minute adding to the buildup.

The housekeeping staff at the far end bent to salute, Mayank noticed irritably. He was consumed. That one taste of her had made him want more, the whole of her, the way he had once had her. In his arms, under him, one with him.

How he hated her dress then, the zip was playing truant, Ish would murder him if he even dreamt of ripping that thing apart but he would if this nasty little thing didn't come off in a minute, he groaned. It obliged finally!

Mayank soaked in the splendour of her body, but only for a minute because he was in a hurry ... all that time he had wasted, those years gone in vain. He devoured her like a ravenous animal. Their lovemaking was frenzied. It had an urgency to it only they could understand, their hearts thumping as one as they blended into one another. The loud noises could have woken the neighbours but they were all at the party.

THE PARTY!

Mayank snapped back into reality.

They didn't talk as they dressed back to their clothes. Mayank tried to discipline his tousled hair but to no effect. Ishiqa was amused. 'He is afraid of her,' she concluded. And now, she was too ...

Santorini

PORT DAY

Cruise ship
2020

They were docking for the night at Santorini. The port was popular. Innumerable Hollywood and Bollywood movies had been shot here. Santorini is essentially among the top romantic destinations of the world ... They all agreed that Santorini was rightfully called 'The Postcard Island'. It was unanimous that the resplendent sunset from atop the village Oia was worth the hype.

Santorini turned out to be a heady concoction of sleepy beach towns and quaint villages, upping the cultural quotient of this stellar island were the sundry archaeological sites. The village of Fira, together with Oia, Imerovigli and Ferostefani, was perched atop the cliff, making up the so-called Caldera's Eyebrow or the Balcony of Santorini. From here, one could

Santorini

soak in the vibrant views of the deep blue sea and the rugged cliffs.

Blue-domed churches, whitewashed cubiform houses, quaint windmills and the ravishing charm of the twin villages of Oia and Fira, is what lends Santorini an ethereal feel. Santorini boasts of spectacular black, white and red sand beaches. However, they were warned against the lava pebbles, and they had to be prepared to walk down a lot on their course to the beach. The mesh of narrow streets and small buildings, each with its characteristic basement housing, told them a history of guarding the town against pirates.

Santorini had something for everyone—from the artsy to the adventurous, from the foodie to the shopaholic. Markets, art galleries, beach shacks and charming cafes lent a cosmopolitan vibe to the island. After a tour to the upper Oia village, they decided to go slow for the day. Santorini would be there tomorrow for them to explore. They found a perfect little black sand beach to spend the rest of the afternoon they had had the foresight to get some lunch packed from the kitchen at the ship. The wine and cheese they had gorged on earlier had only worked up their appetites.

Mahi lay there on the sand, propped up on her elbows, her eyes well hidden behind oversized Gucci shades. The cloying heat was too much to bear and the suntan lotion (she had so generously applied it) seemed to be ineffective. She was in no mood to even lift a finger, but her thoughts travelled, not making sense at all, with no speed breakers to stop her. She kept trying to harness the dervish dance of her thoughts, which were unwilling to hold her hand; their fluid flow was unharnessed, threatening the floodgates to open and sweep her to a faraway land, a land she had once known, where she was the princess who had met her charming prince, where love blossomed and they belonged.

Zorawar had gone further up the forest trail to explore while Hiya and Ahana spread a sheet on the sand and laid down their picnic basket. Samar and the others were still out playing in the cold water at the end of the beach. Poorvi had decided not to join them today, and truth be told, no one was missing her.

Food was out. Ripe peaches, tomato and cucumber sandwiches, honey, fresh bagels and a slab of brie. They even got a tea cake and a bottle of red wine to wrap it all up. Mayank and Ish were nowhere to be seen as everybody made their way to the picnic spread. Zorawar had come back with a bouquet of wild flowers for Hiya, and the rest returned with wet towels and monstrous appetites. Samar scooped Kian into his arms and planted a kiss on his cheek; the two were talking animatedly about something in French. Mahi tried to make some sense of it, of this, of them.

But she just sat there, like someone held up in the lounge, waiting for the doors to open and let her in.

'Say cheese!'

She was jolted back as another great moment was being

captured to be nicely tucked away in the trunk full of memories. She sighed and plastered a full-blown smile for effect.

Poorvi

Santorini, Port Day

Cruise ship
2020

She had stayed back while the group ventured out to the port. The morning was interminable. The medicines were making her fuzzy. 'Rain check,' she smiled disingenuously as Mayank gave her a deep and long stare, sizing up the whole situation. Finally, he shrugged his shoulders and walked away.

If only she had felt a little less broken.

Her usual pugnacious attitude was missing. It must have been the alcohol … or was it the medicines? she pondered as she slid back into the blanket.

It was around lunch that Poorvi woke from her slumber. Her head still hurt but she had time; she threw on a robe and drifted towards the spa. 'Nothing a good massage and a strong brew can't cure,' she decided.

Poorvi

Ish's signature in the register caught her eye as Poorvi took the pen to fill her details in. Ish and Aadi, in the spa together, she smirked. So much for friendships and commitments. Poorvi was amused, but no, not surprised. She could see that Ahana and Aadi weren't the perfect couple they wanted everyone to believe they were. As for Ish, well, she was nothing but a man-eater.

She could hear hushed voices and muffled laughter as she lay on the heated lounger to soak in the oil. She lay there, listening. She recognized the voices and her body grew stiff. The first voice belonged to Ish, but the other faint husky tone that resonated along made her choke. She walked towards that lavender sauna in a trance. She hesitated, just for a second and then, in a flash slid open the door. Lavender mist filled her nostrils. Her body, Ish's body glistened—was it the water or the oil that the sun rays picked? There beside her, beside Ish, sat Mayank, his legs supporting her tiny frame, his hands obscuring her round firm breasts.

There was a short meaningless pause. Ish suddenly stood—disoriented, mortified.

Poorvi was a person in a thousand pieces.

She could not steer her eyes away from the scene splashed out in front of her. Maybe this was what she deserved, she thought, what with all the lies and deceit she had lived through and the lives she had screwed up.

She had never undermined her capacity to sting and spite; she was vile, she knew, but she could hide it all under the veneer of friendship.

'Really?' she snorted in disgust even as Ish reached for her robe. 'You uppity little tramp,' hissed Poorvi. Mayank faltered and stumbled in the process of getting up; his nakedness splashed over Ish's. Mayank steadied Ish and caught her eye, silently conveying that he would handle it—all of it.

Poorvi was hysterical. She could punch him in the face, knock him down for good for all she cared. Her voice had taken on a screeching, jarring quality and all Mayank wanted was to escape that room. He mustered the strength to finally speak. 'Go to your room, will you? I will come in a minute. Don't create a scene here. We will talk about this. Okay!?'

Poorvi met his eyes, challenging. There was nothing there.

She was his nemesis, Mayank knew that, and she would make sure that he knew that.

'We will talk about this, please.' He rubbed his forehead nervously. Ish was still inside that darned lavender sauna, her sobs driving daggers through his heart.

Who had he become?

Here was his wife, standing and crying in front of him, his infidelity exposed and yet his heart smote for Ish. All he wanted was to go and take her in his arms and tell her that all would soon be better.

Poorvi & Mayank

Cruise ship
2020

'May I?' Mayank gestured towards the empty seat at the table. Poorvi was having her lunch; surprisingly, the wine lay untouched. She swirled her spoon through the salad, but even the feta seemed unappetising to her.

'Knock yourself out,' she said, but she was in no mood to indulge him. Poorvi absent-mindedly rearranged the things on the table—straightened a fork, twirled the empty wine glass; all the while, her thoughts were in a distant land, in another time.

The elephant in the room was growing larger.

'You wanted to talk …' There was a faint semblance of a question in his words.

'I'm ready to yell,' she retorted, her calm demeanour evaporating into thin air. 'You have the balls to come barging in and dredging this up.' The shrill tone in her voice hurt his ears. They had been bickering from the start. The cracks in their relationship had been evident from the very beginning. Her temper, her tantrums, his filtered emotions, the silent treatment, and now, the heated arguments; the ghost of Ish had never left Poorvi and Mayank alone. It was the three of them in this relationship, and now the ghost was threatening to come alive.

'I want a divorce,' Mayank said brutally. He wanted to rip off the band-aid in one swift motion. His face held no expression, his eyes gave nothing away. He didn't want to get lost in her melodrama once again. Poorvi shoved the cold pasta down her throat.

'Well played,' she said wryly.

It looked as if she had nothing more on her mind than deliberating about whether to visit the famed blue-domed churches of Santorini or to take a bus to the black sand beach further ahead. She didn't look like someone whose whole world was about to collapse in this moment. Mayank always found this blow-hot–blow-cold attitude of Poorvi unsettling. He could never understand her; he never knew how to respond to a situation. She was unpredictable, and even her impulsive responses seemed to be part of a well-planned diabolic scheme now. And this sudden calm that had enveloped her triggered the alarm bells in Mayank's head; he had been duped once and then many times over.

'Don't be a moron,' she chided. 'Let's try and thrash things out. A moment of lust cannot take away the years we have

Poorvi & Mayank

had together. She cannot take away our marriage.' Poorvi was almost pleading now. From raging fury to outright misery, she was riding a see-saw of conflicting emotions. It made her feel inadequate. He made her feel inadequate. 'Be done with this little misadventure of yours, get her out of your system, even if it takes a couple more of those spa sessions of yours. I will forgive you.' Now she was blabbering over mouthfuls of tasteless and rubbery aglio olio.

He could see the vileness in her eyes; her whole demeanour was off-putting, her blabbering made it worse. He no longer wanted to be in the same room with her. Punch drunk with inexplicable fatigue, he wanted to just walk away from all this drama. He did not want to go down that emotional rabbit hole again. Poorvi gave him a disapproving glance as he plucked a cigarette out of the packet.

'We married each other. It was wrong, it couldn't have been a worse decision then either. But we stayed together all these years when we shouldn't have, making things worse. Another delay in giving us a clean break will take things down a pit ... I do not want to see it. So, no. No, I am not going to stay in this rot. I am not going to let you trick me into a relationship I don't want—one I never wanted,' Mayank stated in a lugubrious tone.

Mayank was pushing her away. Poorvi wasn't even listening.

'Don't ... don't do this,' she was crying hysterically. 'Don't go dark on me!' The sun was briefly obscured by a shadow, a shadow threatening to usurp the life she had built for herself.

'—I should go.' He could not take her dramatics any longer. He wanted to cut loose of her. He didn't want to get sucked into that darkness once again. His usual blasé attitude was driving Poorvi mad.

'No!' she said explosively. 'You don't get to walk away from me just like that. You can't walk out on us ... US! Her hands were now on her belly, protectively caressing. His gaze followed her hand as he stood there nonplussed.

They stood there. The moment seemed like eternity.

Finally, he mustered the strength to speak, still unsure of what to say and how to react.

'What, when ...?'

How could this be possible? His thoughts were muddled. He stammered, not knowing how to put it all together. His mind was playing tricks, he was sure.

'A baby in seven months' time, and last I know, you do understand how babies are made.' She laughed dryly. Mayank moved in closer, touching her belly now. He felt emotions he didn't understand.

'Shall I fix you a drink?' She didn't wait for an answer as she uncorked the bottle and poured red liquid into the goblet. Mayank was ready to cave in once again. Poorvi revelled in the knowledge.

Samar & Mahi

Cruise ship
2020

Samar was leaning against the rails, deep in thought, oblivious to all the hullabaloo around them. A darkness hid behind his eyes. He looked ridiculously handsome, not in conventional terms but his deep brooding looks, which had since long replaced the boyish charm he once exuberated, were enough to stir Mahi's meticulously buried feelings of longing.

'A penny for your thoughts?'

He had not seen Mahi approaching. His eyes gave away nothing away but she could catch the tenderness in his voice. 'Ra … Rachelle …' He cleared his throat, trying to shake away the quiver there. 'Rachelle, loved coming to Lindau,' he managed to complete the sentence somehow.

Mahi knew that Samar was finally ready to talk about his dead wife. And while Mahi wanted to listen, it was painful for her to see the man she loved so much—in love with someone else, someone who was absent and still present between the two of them. 'I am in competition with a ghost,' Mahi had confided in Ahana, 'and I am not winning any time soon.' She sighed. 'Damaged goods'. She understood the true meaning of the phrase probably for the first time in her life.

'She loved it there … at Lindau,' Samar continued. "The lighthouse beckons me," she used to say.'

Mahi was reminded of a story they had learnt in sixth grade called 'The Foghorn'; she instantly understood why Samar had indulged Rachelle in her lighthouse fantasy. It was a melancholy, a loneliness that only lovers could understand. 'She would often go up those winding and narrow 110 steps of the lighthouse to wave at incoming ships … while I waited at the promenade with a gelato, ready for her to consume it. I never went all the way up along with her.' He smirked, as if the sentence held deeper meaning. 'She went away, forever, and somehow, Lindau has seemed like the only place where I could keep her close to me, even if it were just within memories.'

'I can still see her feeding pretzels to the ducklings. A whole two euros worth of pretzels going down the tummies of those gluttons.' Samar was complaining but the warmth in his eyes didn't escape Mahi's attentive gaze.

'I have since retraced her steps, all of those narrow precarious 110 steps, right up to the top of the lighthouse. She told me she inscribed our names—"yours and mine etched on one of the walls there, you have to find them for me"—she was excited when she returned from one of her trips to the tower. I was furious with her for vandalizing a heritage site. "You can be put to task, fined, sued ..." I had admonished. "But everyone was doing it too ... and it has now become a part of our heritage, our story ... the lighthouse is our beacon of love and light", she had said to me. She had had her puppy face on and I could no longer be angry with her.

'I have searched through the lettered walls since—like a maniac, Mahi—day after day going to find that piece of our story, and when I finally found it, the heart with her name beside mine, it was like I found her again.' Tears gathered at the well of his eyes, threatening to breach the dam any second.

Castles of her dreams were now prisons of his mind. They stood there in silence, Mahi and Samar. The waves suddenly seemed larger, whiter, fiercer. A perfect storm.

He could hear Rachelle splashing in the water. Mahi could hear her own heart riffing like the sea, exploding. Mahi was drowning; her heart, unbeknownst, had opened the doors to doom again.

The waves were pulling her down and the only person who could rescue her from such a vortex was standing beside her with a rope around his neck, a rope of shadows that threatened to choke him and take her along.

Cruise Games

Cruise ship
2020

Samar wasn't spending as much time with Kian as he had intended to, but Kian didn't seem to notice. He had so many aunts and uncles vying for his attention. He was growing particularly fond of Aunt Mahi—her name sounded so much like Maa, Kian thought as his little eyes shut to dream of a land where mommy came to hug him and to tell him his favourite unicorn story. He was chuckling in his sleep as Samar dimmed the lights and adjusted the blanket around his tiny frame.

They had gathered at the cruise theatre for the late night game show. 'It'll be fun,' Ahana had insisted. She was super excited to participate, almost sure of them winning the couples' game, aptly called 'MARRIAGE'. And why shouldn't they? After all, Aadi and Ahana knew each other like the back of their hands. They were the epitome of childhood sweethearts, or so Ahana smugly thought. They seemed to be the perfect couple, the 'it' thing; Aadi always attentive to Ahana's needs, trying to make her every wish his command, Ahana, in turn, playing the role of a doting wife to the T.

Mahi wasn't digging the whole scene. She saw lovey-dovey young couples, middle-aged garrulous ones and some who you could tell by the wrinkles on their face and the bend in their backs, had seen the struggles of life and had survived it all, hand in hand. She didn't belong here. She did not deserve to be here. She better take her sad melancholy ass and drown herself in a pitcher of chilled LIT (Long Island Tea).

'Only tequila shots will relieve you of your misery,' her head hinted. But she stayed.

Samar stayed too, his head bent, and she could not read his eyes. He, like her, was there for Ahana. Heck, even Aadi was there for Ahana. 'Your crazy is contagious,' Aadi would often tell his wife, and she couldn't tell if he was being genuine or sarcastic. Mayank and Poorvi had said something about needing time alone while Ish had been conspicuously missing from action since the morning. It was cruising day, which meant that the shops and casinos on the ship would be open all day, and so nobody gave a second thought to Ish's whereabouts. Hiya was present, but as usual, she was tethered to a book. Hiya was a part of their club, but mostly as a silent participant, hardly joining the conversation. 'Reckon, I'll just watch', was her standard reply whenever asked to join a game of cards or to take a dip in the pool. She was always a part yet aloof. Mahi and Ahana understood this. They knew.

The cruise director was rambling on and on, reading out the names of participants from slips posted earlier in the hour. Then all of a sudden, the floodlights swung to rest on Mahi's unsuspecting face. Everybody around her began to clap boisterously and egged her on to join the group on the stage. And now it was Samar's turn to be embarrassed and bullied by the crowd to alight the stage alongside her.

'Ahana, you scheming little shit,' Mahi silently cursed her friend. A visibly flustered Samar climbed the three small steps to the stage in what seemed like eternity. Samar and Mahi, as it panned out, were chosen to add that extra dimension to the 'couple's game'. They were to represent the unmarried couples, courtesy the overindulgent, unrestrained Ahana, who somehow, always managed to get her way.

The compere set the ball rolling, and began with a few predefined questions about each other's partners. The spouse would, in turn, verify if the responses were correct. It was a compatibility quiz, drafted to check the chemistry and understanding between the selected couples.

'White bougainvillea,' Samar replied.

'Aha! That specific. Right you are!' the moderator whooped.

'Black,' guessed Mahi when asked about Samar's favourite colour. The crowd booed. She smiled—so he still insists it is green. Have you ever met a guy whose preferred colour did not belong to the black or white category?

But Samar's favourite was green, not because it actually

was but because her eyes were that shade. Mahi's eyes were every hue of the emerald forest, green-gold with an amber heart, like somebody had lit a flame in the woods.

'Green. His favourite colour is green,' her words almost came out as a whisper. The crowd cheered but she wasn't listening any more. She could feel the eras rushing past her.

He still remembered it; that was all she could think about. Her eyes were now the colour of French chartreuse, the yellow–green liquor threatening to spill over.

The Scare

Cruise ship
2020

Kian's babble was a welcome distraction from the unease that enveloped the dinner table.

Everyone was focused on the meal in front of them; the clinking of glasses and forks against the plates was suddenly all too audible. Eye contact was being avoided and words failed to form. The tension was tangible and the atmosphere was charged.

None dared to interrupt the entropy.

Ish had been missing from the scene the whole day; Poorvi and Mayank had returned for dinner after being away for most part of the day; Samar and Mahi were still reeling from the after-effects of that seemingly simple cruise game which had stirred up some buried emotions. The quiet was disconcerting. A storm was brewing.

The wind had picked up and ominous clouds were gathering. The waves grew rough and the boat was shaking

The Scare

more than it was supposed to. But what they did not know—a hurricane was building up gradually which would ultimately, bring the whole world to a standstill. The news soon reached them; in fact, they, the cruise passengers, made the major part of the story.

The threat of Covid-19 loomed large. Stories of people collapsing like a pack of cards spread. The outbreak had somehow gained a monstrous form on the ship. They were confined to their rooms, cut off from the other passengers and from the rest of the world. The situation was getting worse. The much-hyped apocalypse was what the world seemed to be heading for.

The ship kept cruising, searching for an asylum, a safe docking site but they had suddenly turned untouchable. No country or town was comfortable with letting them—and with them the threat of the fast-spreading killer disease—in. Greece and Croatia had denied them permission to dock. Over a hundred protesters had gathered at Montenegro port to prevent visitors from disembarking, forcing the police to intervene. The protesters threw stones and bottles at the security forces; the forces responded with tear gas. Permission to dock had to be revoked and the ship continued to sail back towards Venice amid passenger frenzy and panic. Food and supplies were scanty. The staff were infrequent, arriving only after repeated requests, donned in hazmat suits to refurbish emergency needs. They had to clean the rooms themselves. Housekeeping was strongly discouraged from changing the

My Suitcase Heart

bedding. Meditation, yoga, books and memories were their only companions. It seemed like being stranded on an isolated island. They now were learning the exact meaning of VUCA world—a world filled with volatility, uncertainty, complexity and ambiguity. It was a dystopian world.

The whole shebang continued until they finally reached the original embarkation port: Venice. They were informed that the Italian authorities were of the view that it was not possible to transport persons over longer distances while maintaining effective isolation (as required under the 'health orders') and for this reason, they would require that cruisers from outside Europe and other faraway countries undertake isolation themselves. They were to isolate for approximately two weeks in Italy before leaving for their home countries.

They were escorted to the respected quarantine centres by volunteers who arrived in elaborate protective gear and hazmat suits. They were treated like loathsome criminals.

Part 4
HOMECOMING

The New Normal

MAHI

India
2020

The clutter of memorabilia, things she had collected across her extensive travels, adorned the rosewood mantelpiece. The living room mirrored her travels across the globe. It was littered with eclectic souvenirs—wooden masks from Bali, Chinese vases, Venetian murano glass and even Japanese ivory netsuke, all thrown in for effect. The dreamcatchers in her bedroom vied for attention, but Mahi loved spending most of her day in her living room.

This was the room that spilled stories from far and beyond, this was her haven. She didn't mind the busy décor one bit (except, of course, when she had to do the cleaning and dusting herself). Photographs of her travels hung in the narrow gallery leading to the rooms; they were a pleasant reminder of her sojourns.

Mahi hadn't done much since the cruise; there was nothing much to be done. The pandemic had made the non-routine the new routine. Stay-at-home was the new mantra. Work-from-home was exciting for the first few days but the endless Zoom meetings soon lost lustre. Her field wasn't exactly mapped for online interactions. Who would think of travel when flights were grounded, when trains were not operating, when borders were sealed and hotels were almost shut?

Armchair travel could just excite as much and she soon found herself shying away from posting any more of those drool-worthy travel pictures on Instagram. She was no longer focused on the algorithms and social media rankings. It had begun to hurt to see, to remember, to know that for the moment the world needed to heal. It needed to settle down, to breathe and to breathe free. 'Maybe, one day soon, we all will be travelling, and this time it would hopefully be more mindful, full of gratitude for the bounty of nature, of diversity of culture, of the vastness of unfamiliar terrains, of richness of history and our ability to soak it all up. Maybe we all will come to appreciate slow, immersive travel', she hoped.

After the ordeal of the cruise ended, they were taken to a compulsory quarantine facility. No goodbyes, no see-you-soons could be exchanged. They were not allowed to see each other. She was flown back with the other stranded Indians by a special Air India flight. None of it felt real. It was like one

The New Normal

long bad dream which refused to end.

A notice was being plastered on the outer walls of her home as she turned the key to her door. She would have to remain confined within the four walls of her home for another twenty-eight days. No house help would be allowed in, groceries would be supplied at her doorstep and some government representatives would keep monitoring and reviewing the situation.

The next few days were spent in a daze. She ate and slept and bathed and changed in a stupor. She had become a zombie. Her mind was numb; a deluge of shock and loneliness flooding every crevice of her being. Life was paused, everything came to a standstill. It was a time warp.

The shock gave way to guilt as days turned into weeks. The government had classified certain areas as hotspots and containment zones as the disease threatened to spread. Her lane came under the scanner due to her travel history. She was responsible, though unintentionally, for the sealing of the street she lived in. Not that it mattered much. Soon the whole nation was under lockdown; all institutions were closed, all work halted, all outings curbed, flights grounded, trains halted. She was finding it hard to cope and was struggling. She couldn't seem to catch a break.

Mom and Dad were in Chandigarh, the city of pink cassias and mango blossoms, of box stores and open spaces. They did call daily to check on her and she put up a brave front for their sake. Her mother motivated her to try exotic recipes, to read new books or reread an old favourite, she asked after her routine every day, and slowly, Mahi developed one. She began to fall in step with this new rhythm. It was her new normal—working from home, listening to celebrity tittle-tattle, searching for apocalyptic reads, learning French through online classes and shaking a leg to Zumba, feeding the puppy litter peppered all around the neighbourhood. Looking back, the routine was what kept Mahi ticking.

August was wet and grey. She hated the thick smell of receding monsoons and the waterlogged streets. Mornings were interminable, stretching into listless nights. The flaming fins of the gulmohars were dying, the hibiscus blooms went unnoticed. She found herself thinking more and more about Samar.

How he must be doing? she kept thinking. France was in rough waters since all the European countries were hit hard by the pandemic. The spread of the contagion was exponential and showed no signs of receding. She knew that it would be impossible to find any details about Samar on social media; he wasn't the Facebook kind of guy. Ahana and Aadi were still at some undisclosed quarantine facility, which only added to her worries. She was hoping fervently now, hoping that Samar would call her himself, would ask her to come back into his life, call and tell her that he could no longer go on living without her. She could feel his presence in her empty spaces, during the sleepless nights, in unbearable mornings and desperate evenings. It made things a tad better. The moment more liveable, the ground beneath her feet firm.

The phone rang. Somebody was calling on the landline. She ran as if her life depended on it. Samar would always call on her landline before; he must remember that number. She picked up the phone, her heart thudding.

'Hello, I am calling from Auto Loans Pvt. Ltd ... are you using ...' She disconnected the call before the insipid voice at the other end could complete her pitch.

Days slipped into months, summer collapsed into fall. Ahana had called once to let her know that everyone was back home safely. Lockdown had found Mahi delving deep into nostalgia, she now often found herself rifling through stuffy drawers, dusty photo albums and tucked away keepsakes. Postcards from her sundry summers abroad tumbled out from everywhere, along with the gushing memories. She sat on the floor, the tribal patterned dhurrie spattered with pictures—happy colourful photographs with frayed margins. She picked each of them, one by one, vignettes of life, her life ...

'Moments when we are infinite, just stories waiting to be made,' she mused as she plucked out an old picture.

Poorvi at the far end of it, smiling, holding on to Ish's waist, giving nothing away. She knew now that the picture was a farce, far from the perfect world that seemed to exist.

Life was slowly limping back to normal; miraculously a vaccine for the virus had been created, however rushed, and after some initial hiccups, it had proven to be quite effective. The world was bouncing back, cautiously.

She could swear that the landline wasn't ringing in the other room, it was her head playing tricks again. She refused to acknowledge the constant buzz but the caller was persistent. It was Ahana. It had to be her. She could badger you relentlessly until you conceded.

'Hi, wassup?' Ahana was back to her chirpy self. The quarantine, thankfully, hadn't seemed to have marred her enthusiasm. 'Are you ready for another holiday, girrl?' She sounded ecstatic.

Mahi squirmed as painful memories of the last holiday came rushing in. She laughed as Ahana's spirited voice continued. 'Don't worry, it will be a nice, cheerful holiday, I promise. We all deserve it.'

Mahi had her doubts, given their holiday history.

'Mahi? Are you even listening? Pack your bags, babe, cause we are all going to Udaipur.' Ahana's voice grew shriller with every word.

'Udaipur?' Mahi could not quite understand. She was in no mood for a holiday, not that she was swamped with work but she was gradually getting used to this phase of self-isolation. There were no alarm clocks, no getting ready, nowhere to go, no one to meet; it was just her thoughts, her memories and herself.

'Ahana, I am not up to it. Besides, my work has suffered a lot during the lockdown, I can't even afford a holiday.' Mahi tried to think of a better excuse because Ahana was not one to let go easily.

The New Normal

'Mahi! Mayank and Ish are getting engaged and the celebrations are at Udaipur!' Ahana blurted out. 'And you can send your apologies directly to them when you receive the formal invite,' Ahana scolded.

'Wow! Really? That's the most amazing news that I have heard in a long time,' Mahi said, dumbstruck. She was genuinely elated for the two of them. 'What about Poorvi? What ... how did this happen?' Mahi was now curious.

'Poorvi and Mayank are now separated. He's waiting for a formal divorce notice but it will happen. Poorvi would have once again succeeded in her diabolic and manipulative schemes but for Covid. If there is anything that that stupid killer virus has done besides putting nature back on track for a while, is reveal Poorvi's vile and wretched nature. Her fake pregnancy was exposed the minute the health department officials picked us up for quarantine protocol. Mayank, the poor guy, he was so concerned about his pregnant wife and pleaded with the authorities to make urgent and adequate arrangements for the expecting mother. The health officials were quick to inform and assure him that his worries were needless as his "missus" was not pregnant. It could be a false alarm, the sensitive ones tried to console a visibly shocked Mayank.' Ahana paused to catch her breath. 'Mayank and Poorvi never got back together, not after the quarantine. The extended lockdown served as a good ruse for separation. Hence, we are all coming to Udaipur, do you mind.' Ahana's excitement crackled through the phone.

Mahi was already thinking of the dresses she would pack. Matching masks were also an issue; she would need to tackle it in due course. Her online buying spree was now going to come in handy. Samar would obviously be there. Ahana had slipped in that little piece of information casually into the conversation.

Mahi did not want to think about it. She feared that her heart could not handle the rush, the excitement and anticipation. Somehow, this time, their meeting would be different. Something in her was sure of it, or was she being too optimistic?

Retribution

HIYA

India
2021

They had come to India a week before the celebrations were scheduled. Zorawar wanted to catch up with some old friends and relatives and Hiya couldn't say no. She felt much tougher and in control of her emotions, especially with Zorawar by her side. And yet, she wasn't sure how she would react once close to what she called home, but what was actually a house of horrors. She had left all that behind. She was happy in the microcosm that they had created several miles far, far away from her past.

Her cell phone rang. The voice on the other side seemed distant, and the line crackled, threatening to disrupt the conversation even before it began. 'Hello, is that Hiya?' the voice asked nervously.

'Yes ...' Hiya replied, still unsure about whether to have answered that question so promptly.

'Hi, Hiya. I am Trisha. I read your tweet.' Hiya did not know how to respond; she did not want to encourage pestering journalists, those story-mongers; she had not tweeted about her #metoo story to grab attention. It had just felt like the right thing to do—cathartic so as to say. It was her small contribution in spreading awareness about abuse within the confines of the supposedly safe haven called home.

'Listen, I am not interested in talking about it,' Hiya said curtly. How had the caller found her number anyway?

'Please don't disconnect.' The urgency in this stranger's voice was evident. 'Hiya di, I am your cousin. The uncle's daughter. Yes ... and please, I just want to speak with you. I know you have returned to India.' The distress in the girl's voice was evident. Hiya was dumbstruck, she had nothing to do with her uncle or this daughter of his. Had her tweet stirred a hornet's nest?

'Di, are you listening,' Trisha's voice seemed meek and battered. Hiya wanted to hang up but she did not disconnect, could not disconnect. 'Will you come to the Women Cell with me before you fly back?' Trisha was pleading now. 'I have called the 1098 Child Helpline before calling you.'

Hiya was listening now, the phone pressed against her ear.

'What? Why?' she almost barked into the phone.

'Because I am you, Di ... I am living the same hell. Years have passed but he has not changed. He has not spared ...

Retribution

not even his own daughter.' Trisha's voice trembled. 'I had a tough time getting your number and have garnered all the courage I had to make this call. Please, Di, I have no one to support me—to even listen to what I have to say. My mom has turned a blind eye ... she refuses to even acknowledge the rot in the house.' Trisha was inconsolable, weeping with each word.

Hiya had made up her mind. It was time to put a kibosh on his fiendish torture.

Thankfully, Zorawar had some well-placed connections and it helped speed things up. An FIR was lodged at the local police station under the POCSO Act and unbailable warrants were issued against the monster. The mother just watched the proceedings—as if she were an ignorant bystander, still not willing to take sides, too embarrassed to own up to the fact that she had known all along. Hiya tightly held Trisha's hands. She knew that Trisha would be all right now; Hiya would make sure of that.

It was time to say goodbye to this part of her life. She was finally saying goodbye to that helpless girl with her hair tied in vibrant love-in-tokyos and her frock cinched at the waist, the girl who hated frocks because they could be lifted so easily, the girl who was afraid of home, of people and of herself in the mirror. She was finally saying goodbye to her fifteen-year-old self for good.

The tide had come to the shore.

Udaipur

India
2021

Their experience of the majestic Udaipur began as soon as they arrived at the hotel jetty, soon after a comfortable limousine pick-up from the airport. The jetty of the famous Taj Lake Palace, from where you embark on a short boat ride to the middle of Lake Pichola, is a stunning piece of art in itself.

The Royal Guard rushed to fetch them, bringing them under the shade of an enormous traditional umbrella. Rose petals showered over them, hinting at how this trip was going to shape up.

The hotel had been built in 1746 to serve as the palace of Maharaja Jagat Singh II—a summer palace. The hotel was built on an envious location, set on an idyllic island jutting out of the pristine lake. Its decadence and opulence make it one of the most coveted hotels in the world. Its intricately carved pillars, painstakingly embellished Persian glass, expensive crystal,

Udaipur

colourful frescoes and lavishly appointed rooms tell a story of grandeur. An intertwined maze of hallways inspires whispered confessions, telling stories of lovers who must have waited for a secret rendezvous as formidable walls bore testimony to their romance, urging one to write that unfinished saga of love and longing. The palace was a stunning reminder of a bygone era, the resplendent royalty that our history is steeped in. The city fanned out beyond the walls, sharing a glimpse of daunting forts and colourful houses.

The entire party was to arrive till late in the evening. Exhausted, Mahi decided to retire to her room. Ahana, though, was in no mood to leave her alone.

'Just go and talk to him,' Ahana said, straight to the point. 'You deserve this, you two belong, baby. I don't understand why you keep denying that and pushing each other away. Don't fight your destiny any longer, give yourself a second chance.'

She stared at Mahi. 'Oh my god! You have the look of a colossal loser on your face. I can hear the chaos in your mind—should I do it ... what will he think ... will he judge me ...what if he says no... catch a break, girl. Someone needs to go first. Talk before it is too late. Pain is inevitable but misery is optional. We are all allowed to make mistakes, though we should make better ones each time.'

Mahi heard her. Ahana could be really persuasive. Always so put together, always so perceptive, and she knew the right things to say. Mahi had needed a push. She was ready to take the leap, the first step. But first, there was a party to attend and she didn't want to miss out on all the fun that Mayank and Ishiqa had planned for tonight. The engagement bash was the only formal ceremony that the couple had planned. It would be later followed by a simple court marriage as Mayank's divorce with Poorvi had finally been formalized only recently, and not without a hefty alimony. Mayank and Ishiqa still planned to exchange vows with their friends in the audience. They had lined up the Las Vegas wedding shenanigans for their honeymoon.

Jagmandir Palace, the venue of their party, was transcendent, lit with a million diyas and candles, huge mashaals and lanterns lined the path. Even the boat that ferried them to the venue was dolled up with fresh flowers, colourful drapes, fairy lights and the works. Trust Mayank to choose a location right out of a James Bond film for his engagement. Toasts were being raised, glasses clinked, laughter emanated from all around; everyone looked radiant and happy.

'To new beginnings,' Mayank proposed.

'To new beginnings,' everyone chorused.

The music shifted gears and all eyes were riveted on the dance floor. The spotlight was on Zorawar, and unbelievable though it may sound, Hiya; the two were occupying centre stage. They had decided to surprise Mayank and Ishiqa with a performance. Hiya was glowing as Zorawar grooved to '*Mehndi laga ke rakhna*' and they all cheered as she matched Zorawar's enthusiasm and energy, step for step, beat for beat.

Udaipur

Zorawar sat down for a moment to catch his breath and Ahana squeezed his hand as tears of joy and gratitude welled up in her eyes. 'Thanks, buddy. If not for you, Hiya would never have felt this safe and confident. She has emerged from her shell and look how beautifully she has blossomed. You are a hero, my friend.' Zorawar hugged Ahana tightly. He had finally won them over, he was now among friends he could call his own.

It was a long night but nobody wanted it to end; they would remember the music, the food, the ambience for a long time.

'I will tell them about our little surprise tomorrow.' Ahana was buzzing with excitement as she leaned on Aadi's shoulder. She was having a hard time keeping it a secret but the two of them did not want to overshadow what was Mayank and Ishiqa's day. 'Let them have their moment, their time in the limelight,' Aadi had suggested, and she had agreed.

A day trip to Devigarh Palace had been planned and they were to take three different cars for the tour. 'The surprise will have to wait till lunch.' Ahana was impatient. She wanted to confide in somebody before she exploded, but Aadi made sure to cling on to his wife lest she spilled the beans. Lunch at the palace was a lavish affair; they were served traditional Rajasthani food in silver thaalis or platters, they gorged on the scrumptious gatta curry, dal baati choorma, ker sangri, laal maans and delectable rose-infused phirni (which was simply ambrosial).

Ahana had found the right opportunity once everybody was satiated and relaxed, after a good meal and with a drink in hand. She decided to break the news. She stood up, gushing with excitement, gestured for Aadi to join her, her eyes dazzling with exhilaration; she was happy and her joy knew no bounds.

'Aadi and I, we are adopting a baby,' she let it out. There were gasps of surprise and then cheers of joy and exuberance. Everyone was elated but a little surprised at the sudden decision. A champagne bottle was uncorked open to celebrate the news and the bubbly worked its magic.

Ahana steered Mahi a little away from all the bonhomie and cheer, she needed to confess to her and fill her in with all the deets. 'It isn't sudden. We have been through our share of heartache and misery. We just decided to give ourselves another chance before everything fell apart.

'The pandemic and its effects all around the world, with medical infrastructure collapsing, the elderly left to die because they could not be saved, town after town becoming ghost settlements, the situation back home where people were walking miles without food or water braving heat and authorities just to be with their loved ones, so many dying without anyone to light their pyre and so many committing suicide because they were lonely and trapped or losing everything they had built—it made us rethink what our priorities were, it made us thankful for what we had and what we could become. Gratitude, hope and patience is what

Udaipur

allowed us to survive.

'With so much uncertainty and disruption surrounding our lives, we could not afford to lose precious moments sulking over what was lost and was beyond our control. With time on our hands and also such precariousness about the next moment, gnawing thoughts that these could be our last moments together, made us sit back and take stock of where we needed to go from here—if we were lucky enough to escape and survive. And I knew what we needed to do, what Aadi and I would love to be. We wanted to bring home another life, to nurture, to parent, to share our abundance and love with someone.

'We will go straight to Mumbai from here and bring Ruhi home. Yes, that's her name, the little one we are bringing home, my soul and the reason for my being.'

Ahana had opened her heart out to Mahi. She added, 'And that is why I also keep telling you to not let this opportunity go. You need to breach the walls and reach out. I know my brother, he will torment himself for an eternity but he will not reach out, as if paying penance. Talk to him and save him and your relationship from doom, Mahi, before it is too late.'

Mahi glanced across the table. They all had come a long way from being huddled in that school canteen over shared aloo patties and lemon soda, with champagne flutes in their hands. Today, after ages, they looked as happy, as carefree as in the days of yore. She caught Samar's eye, he seemed relaxed but distant as usual, isolated, an island. Mahi wasn't too sure but she didn't want to not try, she would not let love slip away once again. She wanted to reclaim her life but she didn't quite know if she had the courage to make the first move.

The evening was balmy and Mahi took her time, labouring to line up her haphazard thoughts. She braced herself, finally ready to face him and tell him that she still loved him as madly, as passionately—for as they say, 'Unless it is mad, passionate, extraordinary love, it is a waste of time'—and that she did not want to waste even a single minute of her life away from him. Her hair scooped up in a messy bun, the stray strands begging to be tamed, her lips painted rouge, matching the flush on her cheeks, and her eyes brighter than the gold selvedge of her dress, which shifted like liquid silk as she walked; the colour agreed with her.

'Blue becomes you, it brings out the colour of your eyes,' Samar had once said, back when he was hopelessly in love with her, when he didn't need to think through the words he shared with her, back when they dreamt of a life together.

The path leading to the porch was lined with beetroot pink and lavender lagerstroemias, the feathery flowers in full bloom. How she loved everything pink, how he disliked anything that colour. The trellis was strung with fairy lights and it formed a canopy of twinkling stars over their heads.

'Hey,' she called out, summoning a smile as her heart raced wildly like a carriage hurtling down a treacherous hill. 'Be still, my beating heart,' she whispered to herself. Had he picked up the vibe or was she about to commit a rookie

Udaipur

mistake by approaching first?

The words hung, like ripe fruits on a bough waiting to be plucked; she was trying hard to keep her voice neutral. He, as usual, was fluent in silence. The evening was warm as the sun went down beyond the hills, the sky shimmering liquid gold like honey treacle. Her mind sifting through an endless carousal of possibilities. Tiny ripples ruffled the surface of the green lake as they stood on the patio, gazing into nothingness and beyond. The occasional call of the birds broke the ticking silence between them.

Drifting apart had been organic and inevitable. The year just after college had been crucifying—they had both had something so integral taken away, it threw them completely out of gear. Chaos had slipped in unnoticed once they had left the warm confines of the iron gates of an institute and were thrown into the cold grey of real life. They had been busy, trying to find the balance and life had gone by, unnoticed. Mahi longed for those times again, when the days held endless promise and the nights came with twinkling dreams, she longed to feel whole again, for Samar to fill the vacuum inside her because no one but him had the power to do so. The longing had multiplied by millions on seeing him again. Is it really true ... what people say about childhood crushes? That you can never outgrow it, that you can never forget your first love? Nothing had changed, yet everything had.

Mahi was coiled up tightly—one look, one sweet gesture and she was set to explode. A crackle of electricity coursed through her body every time he as much as looked at her. He held out a Thumbs Up can for her to share. She gladly took a swig.

'Everything all right?' he asked.

'Yeah, peachy.' The sharpness in her voice suggested otherwise. The drink tasted insipid. Samar stared at her for a long time, searching for answers. She held his eyes for a moment, then dropped her gaze.

He hesitated, seeming to weigh his words. Maybe he was trying to seem nonchalant, trying to act casual. His flushed cheeks and trembling hands gave it all away. 'I am so used to living life caught in the binary—black and white, right and wrong, containing my life in boxes of my own making—but you … you confuse me, you keep me wondering. When I am with you, it all seems to come together. I love you, Mahi but …'

Samar was still gazing into the abyss.

She had heard somewhere that if you gaze long enough into the abyss, the abyss would gaze back at you. But her heart was now sinking. She hated the 'but' which had somehow overshadowed the fact that Samar had professed his love for Mahi.

'I don't really know,' Samar continued. 'What happened with us is not like a skinned knee, you can't just kiss and make it better.'

He was pushing her away again.

'Our life, the ideas and hopes, the dreams and expectations, it is all a gossamer cloud. It takes only a moment to shred it to tatters or blow it all away. Maybe we'll find our way back to each other, maybe not. Maybe this is just the end of a long chapter and not our story. Only time will tell …' Samar was willing himself not to cry. What he felt for Mahi was undeniable, but was he doing right by Rachelle's memory? He knew that Rachelle would have wanted for him to be happy. He understood that life was more about rewriting things, not just writing, but his guilt kept him from acknowledging his feelings. How could she compete against that?

The hollow feeling in the pit of her stomach threatened to usurp everything around her and beyond her. Tears of hopelessness rolled down Mahi's cheeks. She could see it all slipping away, the life that they had once envisaged. They stood there in silence, enveloped in the knowledge of some precious moments strewn around and yet felt so distant, like billet-doux from another world, a faraway land, where they had once been, giggling, dancing, laughing … together.

Sharp voices from the direction of the corridors broke their reverie. Exhausted, they walked away, once again in different directions.

The Café Plan

India
2021

It was their last day in Udaipur. Samar was going back to Lindau. Mahi was feeling lost. She was tired of following him through countries, beyond oceans, across seasons, over the years.

She gathered her thoughts. She still had a sunset cruise and a dinner to get through and she would not let the chaos in her heart show; her agony and pain were hers alone. The dark shadows beneath her eyes told their own tales. She pulled at her hair with swift hard strokes as she got ready, downright savagely, as if the physical pain would alleviate the pain burning inside her. Inside her, a volcano simmered, ready to blow her to smithereens.

The sun was kissing the land farewell for the day and the sky turned into a dynamic gallery; the clouds and the sun played with unhurried strokes, creating a breathtaking

The Café Plan

palette of colour and form. The balmy waters of the lake stood witness to this eternal love affair between the flaming orb and the yonder canvas. Mahi could not bear it any longer and rushed to the jetty as soon as the cruise boat docked.

She missed a step. A thud. Then a loud splash!

She was drowning.

She flailed, flapping her hands desperately and fortunately, she found a rope fastened to the jetties and held on to it for dear life. She could hear alarmed voices now. Samar was trying to tell her something, he held out a hand to reach her but she was too frightened to react. A few second later, the divers from the boat came to the rescue. She was hoisted back to safety, bleeding, cold and shaken. She had bruises and was visibly distressed but it was nothing a warm drink and a painkiller couldn't cure. She retired to her room under the close watch of Ahana, after the required first aid had been administered.

'Promise. No more cruises.' Ahana tried to lighten the mood once Mahi was tucked into bed with a hot water bottle. Mahi could only smile weakly, her mind in a daze and her body hurting in places she hadn't known existed. Ahana closed the door quietly as the medicines finally worked their magic on Mahi and she slipped into a dreamless slumber.

'She is okay,' Ahana reassured Samar. He had been waiting, had refused to budge from the door to Mahi's room.

A few hours later, while toasts were being raised and champagne glasses clinked to celebrate Mayank and Ish's union, Samar was sitting beside Mahi in her room. 'I could have lost you ... again,' he began. For once, Samar was not in control of his feelings. The accident had affected him more than he could fathom. He was suddenly very afraid. In that one moment, when he had witnessed Mahi drowning, he had realized that he could not bear to lose her again. He had felt so helpless in that moment, like being stabbed through his heart, he could not afford to be hurt again.

'Come with me,' Samar pleaded. Mahi was still disoriented from the incident and she believed she was hallucinating. 'Not to Lindau. To Goa,' Samar continued. 'I have some land in Goa, bought it for a song and have been planning to set up a small resort there. I have thought this through. Kian also needs to be nearer to his grandparents and now, with Ahana and Aadi adopting a child, they should be relocating too.' Samar was now rambling. 'Come with me, Mahi. I need you, I love you, God ... I love you so.' He kissed her softly as he continued to speak, things she was not listening to any more. She could feel the chains that held them apart finally dissolving as she melted into his arms.

Mahi was repacking her suitcase, she retrieved her heart, which had been neatly folded and tucked away somewhere inside it. She would wear it again, for her heart, her suitcase heart, had finally found its home.

Epilogue

She reminded him of the mountains and sometimes of the sea, bountiful and serene, deep and ever so restless.

She loves the mountains. And she swears by the sea. So why not give her a slice of both? Samar had booked the exclusive Hurtigruten Cruise voyage, which claimed to cover the spectacle called the Aurora Borealis, the Northern Lights, on its extensive itinerary through the fiords of Norway. He had deliberately selected a cruise for their journey, he wanted to make a fresh start.

'Paris will remain a surprise till the very last, the cherry on the cake,' he mused while getting the tickets and organizing. He wanted to make their honeymoon special, to make up for all the time they had lost, he wanted to make memories that would overshadow the grief of the past. 'I am being unfair to her.' Samar nodded vigorously, as if shaking the dark thoughts away. All he wanted now was to start his days with her smile, to feel the warmth of her body next to him every night. He wanted to build a cocoon impervious to this bitter

Scandinavian cold, to take her in his arms and hold her so tight that nothing could come in between them ever again. He wanted her to be his; he wanted that chestnut mop of hair, those limpid eyes, that supple mouth ... Ah! Yes, all this and more. He could never have enough of her.

Mahi tossed and turned in bed like the princess who couldn't sleep. She could count the imaginary peas spangled beneath her mattress, only they didn't hurt her but they teased her to get out of bed. The skies had begun to change their colour, she could sense that through her half-hooded eyes. They were sailing somewhere around Tromso, their fifth day of an uneventful sailing (strictly in reference to the skylit sightings here, for her life seemed to be crackling with action lately).

Dragging herself out from their toasty bed, she tiptoed out into the balcony. The sea seemed quiet on this cloudless clear night. The cold had an edge; shivering, she adjusted her robe. Her eyes caught a faint green glow that had begun to appear on the horizon. And soon, that whisper of a colour exploded into the night sky with the dazzle of a dancing billow. The sky was on fire.

He caught her at the waist, her hair smelled of wood apples—or was it strawberries?—he could never tell. 'Mahi.' He pulled her towards him and bent down to kiss her full mouth. The celestial shower blessing their union.

Was she dreaming again? She pinched herself.

Acknowledgements

This is no piece of award-winning literature, I admit and accept this much. But it has a part of my heart and I thank the readers who picked it up; some to dig deeper, others to slice it finely into nothing where we all eventually belong

But before that, I would like to thank my husband, Jeetender, not a trite, cliched thank you but a thank you for being my axis, for making my heart skip a beat and making my mind take a leap, for taking me places and keeping me anchored. He gives me ideas and shows me the path, he makes me dream and lives to fulfil those dreams. I would also like to mention my son, Kushagra, who constantly motivates and pushes me to stretch my boundaries; he is my forever admirer and in-house critic. My sister Divya and my mom who are a treasure trove of stories and their vocabulary is something I am envious of. They are the motivation and the inspiration. I finally get to thank my friend, my beta reader, my soul sister, Sonia, the only one whose advice I listen to and sometimes act upon too. A big bow to my grandparents, who must be smiling from somewhere amongst the stars because it was they who introduced me to the contrasting world of Noddy and *Dharamyug*.

Finally, this is for my dad, who might not understand my choices but has always been there to support my decisions, propel my initiatives and to remind me that he has my back. And though I am far from churning out a Booker prize winner, I do hope that I have done my father proud. I may not be at the top of the game, but I haven't stopped walking in that direction and that walk started with the first step he taught me to take.